Batsheva's Wonder-Weave Jewish-Themed Verse

by

Barbara Hantman
Illustrations by Esther Leiper

DORRANCE
PUBLISHING CO
EST. 1920
PITTSBURGH, PENNSYLVANIA 15238

Dorrance Publishing Co
585 Alpha Drive
Suite 103
Pittsburgh, PA 15238
Visit our website at *www.dorrancebookstore.com*

ISBN: 978-1-4809-4295-0
eISBN: 978-1-4809-4318-6

For the noble NEW YORK POETRY FORUM whose members meld the soaring of mind and heart— a place where I have been allowed the privilege of giving seven lectures on the intersection of Judaism and the art of poetry.

TABLE OF CONTENTS

ACKNOWLEDGMENTS xi

I. HALLELUJAH, HOLIDAYS! 1

    Master of Pardons, Answer Us! (English version) 3

    Master of Pardons, Answer Us! (Hebrew version) 4

    Lunes for Rosh Hashanah 5774 5

    Four Shofar Cries 6

    Apprehend the Ram's Horn! 7

    Teshuva: A Sacred Turning 8

    Our Given Fates 10

    High Holiday Hymn 11

    O King of Grace, Cleanse Us! 12

    Yom Kippur: Time of Penitential Awe 13

    Sukkoth: Holiness of Nature's Bounty 14

    Sukkoth Falls in Autumn 16

    Sukkoth: Nature as God's Delight .17

    Sukkoth: Sheltering Under the King's Canopy 20

    Simchat Torah Begins 22

    Simchat Torah: Glorious Wedding 24

    Simchat Torah Enchantment 26

    Simchat Torah in Liozna 28

    Chanukah: Festival of Jewish Singularity 30

    The Dreidel Game 31

    Chanukah Villanelle 32

    Chanukah Reflection 33

    Tu B'Shevat: Fruit of Redemption .35

    Under God's Sacred Canopy 36

    Purim Shpiel: Delight of Triumph .38

No More Hamans! 40

Purim: Masks Donned and Removed 41

Purim: Joy of Divine Unmasking 43

Purim Pantoum: Esther's Request 44

Passover Libation 45

Pesach, Matzoh, MAROR! 47

Passover: Let the Unfettering Begin! 49

Passover Bouquet 51

Anticipating Shavuot 52

Shavuot: Pesach Perfected 54

Shavuot: Celestial Breakthrough 55

Batsheva's Kinot 56

Only One-Day Tisha B'Avs: Sight, Hearing, Voice Recovered 59

Tisha B'Av: Sorrow in Summer 61

II. IN A PIOUS MOOD 63

Priestly Raiment 64

After Candle-Lighting Prayer 66

Prayer for Peace in the Levant 68

Divine Intervention 69

Transcendence 71

The Cloak of Faith 72

Mighty Fifty 73

Post-Surgery Genuflection 75

The Holy Fabric 76

Bardic Drumbeats 77

III. RIGHTEOUS WARRIORS 79

Moses: Mission and Demise 80

Brother Soldier 82

When the Righteous Were Outnumbered 84

The Purple Badge of Merit 86

I Shall Sing (English version) .89

I Shall Sing (Hebrew version) .90

Five Earth-Angels 91

Los cinco ángeles de la tierra .92

Israel at 67 94

Wounded Warriors 96

My Brother's Tears 97

Mariner-Reverie at 91 100

Chagall in Crimson and White 101

Twilight Reverie for Jack 103

Name Tribute Sonnet: *George Drummond* 104

H. Heine: Artist-Martyr 105

Widower Bard 107

Savior of Blizzard Jonas 108

Marius, Deserving and Endearing 110

IV. WIVES & LASSES 113

Grandma Lena 114

Ethics of the Mothers 116

Profile and Silhouette 118

El perfil y la silueta 120

Ode to a Teak Desk 122

The Meaning of It All... 124

La significancia de lo todo... .125

Acceptance 126

La aceptación 127

Mother Chides 128

Glossary for "Senior Memory Cascade" Sonnet Sequence . . .129

Senior Memory Cascade I 130

Senior Memory Cascade II 131

Senior Memory Cascade III 132

Senior Memory Cascade IV 133

Senior Memory Cascade V 134

Senior Memory Cascade VI 135

Senior Memory Cascade VII 136

Senior Memory Cascade VIII 137

Senior Memory Cascade IX 138

Senior Memory Cascade X 139

Ninetieth 140

Sonnet for Sarah 141

Sleeping Treasures 142

Los tesoros durmientes 143

Sixty-One 145

Lorelei of Little Neck Bay 147

Others Just Couldn't See... 148

Los otros apenas pudieron ver... 149

Las Desdichadas and the Seasons 150

V.   JEWELS OF CREATION 151

Seasonal Flashback Nonets 152

Little Neck Bay: Now, and Then 156

Autumn Harvest: Season of Kindly Departures 158

The Copper Beech 159

Bayside Winter Scene 161

Gifts of Early April 162

Whitestone Springtime Haiku 163

Than-Bauks for Springtime Flora 164

The Bejewelled World 166

El mundo enjoyado 167

Holy Land Species Villanelle 168

The Godly Gingko 170

In Praise of the Passerine 171

Unicorn and the Herd of Mustangs 173

VI. URBAN VIBES 175

Strawberry Fields Reverie 176

Five and Three in the City 177

Unlovely Proverbs 178

Refranes no preciosos 179

Yiddish Family Traditions Abecedarian 180

Neue Galerie: From Sublime to Diabolical 182

Urban Ethical Will 185

Outer-Borough Paradise 187

ABOUT THE AUTHOR 189

ACKNOWLEDGMENTS

I wish to thank Sabra, Hebrew University graduate and Manhattanite Michal Nachmany for proofreading and typing up, with Hebrew vowels included, poems I originally wrote in Hebrew script.

Thanks are also due Dr. Pedro Gil, a Galicia native ("gallego") and math teacher of excellence at Flushing High School for proofreading my Spanish verse. Driver Marcos Loaiza also pitched in with corrections, and got me to and from work on time in all kinds of weather. In the teacher's room, Mrs. Oveida Martinez made suggestions to improve my Spanish writings, also providing a repast of Colombian cheese fritters ("buñuelos").

The following editors have published work found in this volume: Charles Portolano (*The Weekly Avocet*), George Northrup (*Freshet*), Perry Terrell (*Conceit Magazine; Amulet*), Milo Rosebud (*Lone Stars Poetry Magazine*) and Paula Camacho (*Nassau County Poet Laureate Society Review*).

As President of the Fresh Meadows Poets, Dr. Northrup has been the soul of congeniality. As President of the New York Poetry Forum, Mr. Daniel Fernandez has offered witty, insightful feedback and incisive analysis after both lectures and performances.

Other dear poetry colleagues and personalities in the New York vicinity include Mrs. Juanita Torrence-Thompson (retired editor of

Mobius, The Poetry Magazine), Dr. Katherine Hogan of Long Island University, the De Martini's, Fran Radbel Bolinder, Anne Hosansky (retired thespian) and Mr. Harry Ellison of "Harry Ellison's Poet's Circle"—now my treasured Torah study companion.

Finally, multi-talented Esther Leiper of New Hampshire's White Mountains Region has been a conscientious poetry colleague correspondence "pen pal" over the years—taking time from her family responsibilities, rural pleasures and career as a gifted writer to produce apt, vivid color illustrations for my books.

Barbara Hantman
Whitestone, New York
September, 2016

I. HALLELUJAH, HOLIDAYS!

Master of Pardons, Answer Us!

How is it possible to find comfort and acceptance in a complacent world?

Master of Pardons, answer us!

Why does man see the simple exterior and not the interior full of grace?

Master of Pardons, answer us!

When will the strong march hand in hand with the afflicted in joy?

Master of Pardons, answer us!

Where will the crooked places straighten up and offer beams of light?

Master of Pardons, answer us!

Who will convince God that now is the time to welcome the Messiah?

Master of Pardons, answer us!

Master of Mercy, Master of Loving-kindness, Master of Charity:
Answer us with the force and certainty you used to burnish the brightest star.

Selichot before Rosh Hashanah 5774

אֲדוֹן הַסְּלִיחוֹת, עֲנֵנוּ!

אֵיךְ אֶפְשָׁר לִמְצֹא נוֹחִיּוּת וְקַבָּלָה
בְּעוֹלָם שֶׁאֲנַן?
אֲדוֹן הַסְּלִיחוֹת,עֲנֵנוּ!
מַדּוּעַ בֶּן אָדָם רוֹאֶה אֶת הַחִיצוֹנִיּוּת הַפְּשׁוּטָה וְלֹא אֶת הַפְּנִימִיּוּת
מְלֵאַת הַחֵן?
אֲדוֹן הַסְּלִיחוֹת,עֲנֵנוּ!
מָתַי הַחֲזָקִים יִצְעֲדוּ יָד בְּיָד עִם הַמְיֻסָּרִים
בְּשִׂמְחָה?
אֲדוֹן הַסְּלִיחוֹת,עֲנֵנוּ!
אֵיפֹה הַמְּקוֹמוֹת הָעֲקֻמִּים יִתְיַשְּׁרוּ וְיָפִיצוּ אֲלֻמּוֹת
אוֹר?
אֲדוֹן הַסְּלִיחוֹת,עֲנֵנוּ!
מִי יְשַׁכְנֵעַ אֶת הַשֵּׁם שֶׁעַכְשָׁיו הַזְּמָן לְקַדֵּם בִּבְרָכָה
אֶת הַמָּשִׁיחַ?
אֲדוֹן הַסְּלִיחוֹת,עֲנֵנוּ!

אֲדוֹן הָרַחֲמִים, אֲדוֹן הַחֶסֶד, אֲדוֹן הַצְּדָקָה:
עֲנֵנוּ בְּעֹז וּבְוַדָּאוּת שֶׁאַתָּה הִשְׁתַּמַּשְׁתָ לְמָרֵק אֶת הַכּוֹכָב הַכִּי מַזְהִיר.

בַּת-שֶׁבַע הַנְטְמַן--

(8/30/13)

סְלִיחוֹת לִפְנֵי רֹאשׁ הַשָּׁנָה 5774

Lunes for Rosh Hashanah 5774 *

Barb's New Year
Time for mercy's reign –
Jarring clangs.

Honey, seeds:
Pomegranate's blush
Fruitful hopes.

Sarin rage
Land of wheat, groves, oil
Genocide?

Syria
Putin's slit-eye smile
Odd savior.

Acorns drop
Concords, tart Macs, gourds
Fall: heal man!

* These are patterned after the Jack Collum lune (sleeker version of a haiku) with 3/5/3 syllable count.

Four Shofar Cries

"Tehehkiiiaaah!"
Hear the first shofar cry –
Herald for mending one's ways in the New Year,
Clarion call to prayers of Kingship, Remembrance and Revelation.
"She-va-rim!"
Behold the second cry of the shofar –
Three blasts to awaken sleepy reformers
So in need of jolts from a ram's horn of Lordly nobility.
"Teh-eh-eh-ru-u-u-ah-ah-ah!"
Hail, the third shofar cry –
Nine staccato blasts sure to impart energy for introspection and correction,
Allowing betterment of mankind as a gift on the world's birthday.
"Tehehkiiiaaah Gedooooooolahahahah…!"
The final shofar blast is an endless, stupendous outpouring of piety
Emerging from the reverent baal tekiah's pursed lips and cupped palms
As he blows, blows, blows the sacred horn of ingathering, battle and worship
With breath that has been schooled in the art of sacred musical tenacity.

Blessed be all shofars and those who have made them wail, implore, moan and exhort
From Abraham's hospitable desert tent and Moses' soulful Sinai encampment
To synagogues of the modern "Medinat Yisrael."
Forever hold dear the four heavenly Rosh Hashanah whirlwind intonations:
"Tekiah!"
"Shevarim!"
"Teruah!"
"Tekiah Gedolah!"

Apprehend the Ram's Horn! *

In honor of the New Moon-New Year;
With homage to Adam's creation on the sixth day –
Leading to sublime consciousness proven by a penchant for naming
olive trees and ibex –
Invoke jubilation at the birthday of the brown-beige-blue-green marble
world:
Apprehend the ram's horn's bleating-trumpet serenade
When autumn brandishes her leaf-kaleidoscope in the month of
Tishrei!

Shofar cries are like midwives:
They deliver up mankind's hopes and dreams;
Move the King from His emerald throne of judgment
To a silken footstool of compassion;
Remind descendants of forebears' trek on the tiger's eye path
From blinding sirocco to oasis-salvation.

May the Hebrew horn's beneficent blasts heralding Rosh Hashanah
Ever bring the Lord's ruby wisdom to courts of human endeavor.
With Almighty's charity,
Encourage tribesmen to polish neighbors' reputations until they gleam
With a patina of good will.

*Inspired by the Chabad.org online essay, "Rosh Hashanah Un-
wrapped" by Rabbi Tzvi Freeman.

Teshuva: A Sacred Turning *

Straighten from a drooping stance to upright glory of the sunflower;
Shake off copycat mud of mindless material gain;
Remember Revelation and Creation as twin staffs entwined with white
almond blossoms;
Taste the honey of prayer offerings uttered under the blessed wedding
canopy;
Imagine being a servant who brings cedar to the Great Master for the
building of future palaces of golden deeds.

**Do teshuva – sacred turning toward rose of Sharon speech and
red anemone heart!**
**Do teshuva – make a blue-green marble world where once-weep-
ing children now cry out in delight!**

Believe that redemption will sprout in verdant springtime;
Prepare to grasp the awesome finger of God in the Heavenly Court
on wintry
Judgment Day;
Put lustrous crowns of kingship on virtuous heads during New Year
musings –
Let useless old habits perish like curled red maple leaves swirling in au-
tumn winds;
Permit the ram's horn staccato-legato to trumpet Lord's coronation
over a newly-seeded
Eden of goodly intentions.

**Do teshuva – sacred turning toward rose of Sharon speech and
red anemone heart!**

Do teshuva – make a blue-green marble world where once-weeping children now cry out in delight!

* "Teshuva" (Hebrew word for turning toward or returning to a path of righteousness) concepts that inspired this poem were put forth by Rabbi Adin Steinsaltz in his chapter on "Rosh Hashana — The New Year" in his book *Change & Renewal: The Essence of the Jewish Holidays, Festivals & Days of Remembrance* (Maggid Books, Jereusalem; 2011).

Our Given Fates *

On the New Year they are merely Almighty thoughts;
On Atonement Day God's inklings are carefully wrought.
 Who shall bask in descendants' love;
 Who shall search and seek and rove.
 Who will scatter seeds and reap a harvest surplus;
 Who will bear dashed dreams' burden, and keep it hush-hush.
On the New Year they are merely Almighty thoughts;
On Atonement Day God's inklings are carefully wrought.
 Whose perfect vigor will allow pursuit of a myriad tasks;
 Whose frailties will require medicinals poured from flasks.
 For whom virtue will be rewarded with glory and respect;
 For whom chastisement and scorn will be all that's left to collect.
On the New Year they are merely Almighty thoughts;
On Atonement Day God's inklings are carefully wrought.

For some signatories the year's inscribed decree seems harsh, indeed!
Let all broken shards of humanity therefore follow this Lordly screed:
"Repentance, prayer and charity may remove the evils foretold!" –
As Providence knows foibles of person and group to be manifold.
"Improve, live, be worthy of my Image!" He exhorts the downcast or straying –
While Archangels Gabriel, Rafael and Uriel's heavenly harps are playing.
"Ah, man is as ephemeral as a desert breeze –
There's just so much uplifting from his soul to be squeezed!"

On the New Year they are merely Almighty thoughts;
On Atonement Day God's inklings are carefully wrought.

* Inspired by the "Unetaneh Tokef" prayer from the Yom Kippur Day
of Atonement liturgy, cf pp. 530-535 in *The Complete Artscroll Machzor
Yom Kippur*; Translation and Commentary by Rabbi Nosson Scherman.

High Holiday Hymn

(Inspired by Spanish-Hebrew Golden Age poet Yehudah HaLevi's poem, "Hymn for Atonement Day")

Lord, at the New Moon in late summer
Give us strength to blow the ram's horn before You.
Our King, help us celebrate the world's birthday –
Forgive our shortcomings, we plead with You.

Lord, turn toward the cloakless, shoeless and shivering
As they seek warmth from shining Countenance of You –
Our Father, extend to them charity of New Year joy,
For their few comforts flow from You.

Lord, when solemn autumn begins
May we again trumpet the imploring ram's horn for You.
Our Master, heads bowed, a litany of sins we will cry out –
Be our Patient Shepherd, knowing that our splendor must ever stay far
beneath You.

Lord, let famished lips and shrunken pride
Be cleansed by pure waters sent by You.
Almighty, coat our prayers with the sheen of mercy,
Molding our character to better resemble You.
**Lord, embrace us when we bring golden baskets of New Year
gladness;**
Lord, turn not away from our pine needles of Atonement Day duress!

Oh King of Grace, Cleanse Us!

Change a path of iniquity into a righteous way for dust-covered stumblers:

Oh King of Grace, cleanse us!

Mold potter's clay into vessels that pour out kindness and justice rather than gold trinkets:

Oh King of Grace, cleanse us!

Blow blacksmith's bellows to forge a brass love-pledge ring that lacks dross of quick temper's flare:

Oh King of Grace, cleanse us!

Clap chains on the false accuser who makes the righteous seem dastardly and the wicked appear uplifted:

Oh King of Grace, cleanse us!

Nudge your sheep away from dry riverbeds of indifference and toward coursing streams of caring:

Oh King of Grace, cleanse us!

On this Day of Atonement blow shofar staccato and smooth for stained rose purification;
Defeat the serpent to vindicate Moses' beloved, virtuous nation.

Yom Kippur: Time of Penitential Awe *

Set aside ten Days of Awe to prepare for Atonement:
Seek *teshuvah:* return to guilelessness of Adam and Eve gamboling
about fig trees of Eden;
Cling to *tefillah*: words that attach themselves to Godliness like a trellised rose greeting sunlight;
Pursue *tzedakah*: righteousness as strong as bedrock and ubiquitous as sand.

When Yom Kippur arrives, annul soul-choking oaths that squeeze like
a lost lamb's tightening rope collar;
Chant "*Al Chet!*" to humbly pour a ritual bath full of rainwater on a
litany of parched-earth sins;
Allow the closing *Neilah* prayer to mark the Lord's meteor-flash singularity,
As limestone Temple Gates close and sapphire Gates of Heaven lock –
Fixing the earnest penitent's moral fate concerning deeds of veiled
omission and shadowy commission,
Dating from last year's late-autumn harvest of green,
yellow and orange gourds –
Emblems of His rainbow-hued, justice-craving Creation.

*Stanza 1 is informed by Rabbi Jonathan Sacks's Chabad.org online
essay, "Teshuvah, Tefilla and Tzedakah" from his book *Torah Studies*,
an adaptation of the Lubavitcher Rebbe's talks.

Sukkoth: Holiness of Nature's Bounty *

Come, let us celebrate Sukkoth!
A harvest holiday of ancestral joy has been ordained.
Sit and bless a fruit nut bar inside a hut with bamboo walls,
Silver birch branch roof, green-gold-orange hanging gourds,
Auburn ears of dried corn and garlands of ivy.
Wave the Four Species of Holy Land autumnal pride –
East, South, West, North, up, down –
Capturing directions of winds' soul breath and
Magnetism of polar pull wisely put in place by the Almighty.
Clasp fragrant yellow, heart-shaped citron of Torah learning and good deeds,
Gracefully bent date palm branch: spine of scholarship that became a
life obsession,
Myrtle with eye-shaped leaves and aura of Bible mastery,
Willow with lip-leaves that lacks both pious study and righteous practice.

The citron is "esrog": aorta flowing with blood of obedience and love
for His dominion;
The date palm branch is "lulav": expert at bowing and bobbing in beatitude;
The myrtle is "hadas": cantor who intones cherished scroll portions in
ancient humming cantillation;
The willow is "aravah": speaker of psalms and liturgical poems that
bring comfort like a cardinal trilling in snow.
Four Species bounty is truly the gift of God's omnipresence for all nations!
Within the Meeting House of Prayer,
Circle the Torah platform seven times in regal procession,
Brandishing enchanting esrog, noble lulav, demure hadas and wistful aravah.
Then, beat five willow branches on the sanctuary floor –
Thus rubbing sweet balm of Gilead to soften harsh judgments from He
Without End.

Gather grapes, figs, almonds, pomegranates and olives as weather cools,
Remembering to utter a plaintive prayer for rain that will ensure
A burgeoning of wheat, wine and oil after winter downpours.
May never-ending cycles of Sukkoths be seasons of our gladness
Amid nature's hallowed abundance, under God's Sacred Canopy.

*Sukkoth (Feast of Tabernacles) traditions, practices and legends captured in this poem were gleaned from "The High Holidays Guide" (Lubavitch Youth Organization, 2005), *Chageinu* by Rabbi Eliezer Wenger (pp. 71-72) and Philologos's *Forward* article, "A Harvest With Little To Harvest" (9/20/13, Arts & Culture section, p.15).

Sukkoth 5774

Sukkoth Falls in Autumn

Build a booth of bamboo walls and a pine branch roof;
Hang gourds of orange and green-yellow stripes;
Suspend bunches of Concord grapes;
Dangle red Gala apples and green Granny Smiths from semi-see-
through ceiling of green boughs interwoven with burnished autumn
leaves shed by nearby red maples.
Add children's crayon drawings of smiling families breaking bread in a
"sukkah" paradise;
Now the ambiance of ancient desert nomad star-gazing wanderlust has
been recaptured!

Hold steady a fragrant yellow citron;
Shake myrtle, willow and palm frond
Fervently in compass directions –
Also paying homage to each pole.
Remember that plant matter is especially compelling in autumn,
When sepia-brown-gold stalks of dried corn become charming decoration–
Rather than mundane people fuel.

Bless a vegan coconut carob chip cookie and glass of Rothschild Carmel
Riesling in your chilly fall close-to-nature temporary abode:
Recall Sukkoth as a festival of meanderers who found salvation in Zion;
Pay homage to the Almighty before His luxuriant, stalk-shriven decay.

Sukkoth: Nature as God's Delight *

Eat butternut squash soup, apple cake and ambrosia
In a "sukkah" hut with red maple branch roof and green canvas sides –
Hung with Concord grapes, orange gourds and dried reddened-kernel corn.
See stars peek through the crisscross ceiling verdure:
A reminder of Moses as guiding beacon for forty years,
Expertly shepherding Sinai Desert's wandering trudgers.

Gather citron, palm frond, myrtle and willow twigs
For a Four Kinds blessing over the fragrant wise and earth-bound simple:
Wave the lanky lulav, almond-eye hadassim and pliant aravot in six
Godly directions:
Right, left, forward, up, down, backward.
Hold the oval, Gulliver-sized lemon etrog firmly in the left hand,
Frond and twigs in the hand that writes with cunning of eternal love for
Jerusalem's Temple, walls, mikvahs and rainbow limestone.

Remember the ancient Water-Drawing Celebration
When Levites descended broad Temple steps at daybreak,
Proudly bringing their stoppered clay vessels to the Shiloach stream,
Then returning to the sound of blissful trumpet blasts:
Now purifying Sukkoth water could be poured from bronze pots
Onto the awe-inspiring altar of sacrifice –
Connecting the Jewish faith to a gracious Master's joy in sustaining life.

Vegetables and fruits consumed and displayed in
A tabernacle open to heavenly orbs in velvet indigo darkness;
Four Kinds derived from goodly charming trees to treasure;
Euphoria of water libation immersion.
Sukkoth: nature as God's delight!

* This holiday poem for the "Feast of Tabernacles" was informed by Chabad.org essays, including "The Joyous Water-Drawing Ceremony" by Menachem Posner, and by the StudyLight.org essay "Holman Bible Dictionary: Vessels and Utensils."

WORDS FOR SUKKOTH

The willow bends but does not break
Staying limber for the Sukkoth's sake.
If citron's tart; life's not always sweet;
While palm and myrtle together meet
 for the Sukkoth's sake.

Sukkoth: Sheltering Under the King's Canopy*

Forgiveness for the Sin of the Golden Calf
Led to trudgers being guided by Clouds of Glory –
Yet the Lord commanded forty years of desert
meandering and booth-dwelling
For incubation of a new, freedom-minded generation
Meant to someday tend green fields,
purple vineyards and pomegranate orchards
In sacred, post-Eden Canaan.

Each autumn, tabernacles are lovingly constructed
To recapture purifying simplicity
of the ancient tentative trek that fully extinguished slavery.
Bamboo poles hold together yellow canvas for gust-resistant sides,
While silver birch branches and corn husks make a semi-see-through roof–
Ideal for indigo evening star-gazing and contemplation
of a wondrous Maker.

Cradle and shake in the directions of wind, heaven and earth
Four Kinds that capture the delight of trees:
Ample "etrog" citron with sunshine of good deeds and learning;
Lanky "lulav" date frond of Torah insights yet to be applied;
Almond-eyed "hadas" myrtle of untutored beneficence;
Bowing "aravah" willow that weeps over limitations of ignorance.
Hold, bind, grasp blessed fruit and foliage for sublime blended atonement.

Circle the pink marble sanctuary altar with five bound willow boughs,
Then beat them on the mosaic-tiled floor five emphatic times –
Petitioning the Almighty for pearls of Torah wisdom and Abraham's
hospitable ruby heart.

20 | Barbara Hantman

Simplicity of huts for repast and repose;
Poignant bounty and symbolism of fall vegetation;
Memory of God's chastisement via forty vagabond, sand-inundated years:
Another Sukkoth has sheltered a world in need of
The King's universal succor.

* Inspired and informed by the Chabad.org online essay, "Sukkot and Simchat Torah: One Twig and One Leaf" — adapted by Yanki Tauber from the teachings of the Lubavitcher Rebbe, Rabbi Menachem Mendel Schneerson.

Simchat Torah Begins *

Eighteen minutes before mauve autumn sunset,
Kindle two ivory-white Good Day candles –
Making sure that blue-green, gold-trimmed Israeli holders
Stay steady for festival blessing that demands
Piety of covered eyes and arms waving above passion-flame duo.
A white lace veil is respectful head-covering,
Flowing onto practical yet beguiling gray jersey holiday gown.
Tonight's meal requires two whole shiny, egg-brushed challahs;
Stuffed cabbage with raisins will be followed by
Grace After Meals and the Y'aleh V'Yavo prayer:
"May our remembrance ascend and be seen
By the Lofty One who restores His Presence to Zion."

Eager husband and children will enter the carnation-festooned
synagogue in party attire
Ready to be summoned up red-carpeted stairs of spiritual grandeur
To hear inception of Moses' final benediction from weighty,
end-of-scroll Deuteronomy;
Able to gingerly lift four dressed Torahs in their sky blue, royal blue,
maroon and cream velvet splendor,
Then elatedly dance around the recitation platform seven times,
As though this unique, age-old,
life-enhancing gift were a light-as-a-feather boon
Given just five minutes ago at tawny, arid Sinai.
Realize that another Erev Simchat Torah gladsome
beginning has been accomplished
When dear ones return home from star-gazer walk with heavenly smiles –
Wedded to Law that has withstood powerful tempests and perplexing trials.
* Family rituals for the night Simchat Torah begins (Erev Simchat

Torah) are put forth by the National Jewish Outreach Program site Njop.org.

Simchat Torah: Glorious Wedding *

Give "feet" to four Torah scrolls
By prancing around the reading platform seven times:
Cradle the velvet-covered parchments
Like light blue, dark blue, cream and maroon babies
To be nourished with vitamins of tender faith.
Undress the light blue Torah;
Beckon the Bridegroom of Finality
To recite Moses' "This is the Blessing" –
Deuteronomy's poignant closing wisdom.
Roll, roll, roll, roll the dark blue Torah
So that the Bridegroom of Creation
Can intone in baritone, bass or tenor
The Genesis story's mind-rattling week of wonder
That served as Big Bang of the soul.

Call up the children of the congregation
To be honored under black-and-white
Striped prayer shawl canopy:
Bless them in the name of Jacob –
He who triumphed over a wrestling angel;
Patriarch who multiplied like seeds of a pomegranate
While bonded to virtuous sister helpmates of valor.
Prepare a feast of foods shaped like the beloved Torah scroll –
Stuffed cabbages in a raisin-lemon-tomato sauce,
Or apple blintzes from fresh-picked fruit.

Arise! Arise! Arise!
Harken, sons and daughters of Abraham!
The glorious wedding between endings and beginnings of the Law

And their fusion with God's selected people
Has been forged into a profound nuptial contract
For another year of piety and joy.

* Informed by the Chabad.org essay, "Joy That Knows No Bounds: From the Talks of the Lubavitcher Rebbe, Rabbi Menachem M. Schneerson" and from Chabad.org's "Simchat Torah Guide."

Simchat Torah Enchantment *

In early autumn with burnished leaves dangling and swirling
Assign to the Torah Bridegroom recitation
of Moses the ramrod prince's final blessing:

"There is none like unto God, O Jeshurun,
Who rideth upon the heaven as thy help,
And in His excellency on the skies.
The eternal God is a dwelling place,
And underneath are the everlasting arms,"

Then, command the Groom of Genesis
to intone a booming, beneficent account
Of a chaos-shattering Deity's glorious efforts to sculpt
A diadem-world to crown Adam and his kind.

Now it is time to tenderly embrace maroon, blue and beige velvet-clad
Torah scrolls
With their jingling jangling silver pomegranate finials;
To prance past a golden Lion of Judah stained glass window,
One circuit for each day of Creation week wonder.

Give little ones rejoice-with-the-Torah flags to brandish while dancing
in God's sanctuary:
See white doves, spotted deer, King David's polka-dot headdress, lush
Arks of the Covenant with scalloped Ten Commandment tablets nes-
tled above –
All flashing by on green, yellow, red, orange background paper.
Feed toddlers Torah-shaped cookies
with light-blue frosting and purple stars.

Sing delightful Simchat Torah songs of faith and contentment:

Ana Aveda: "I am a servant of the Holy One, blessed is He."
Ashrei Ha'am: "Praiseworthy is the people for whom Hashem is their God."
Ashreinu: "We are fortunate — how good is our portion, how pleasant our lot."
David Melech: "David, King of Israel, is alive and enduring."
Hinei Ma Tov: "Behold how good and pleasant is the dwelling of brothers in unity."
Ivdu Et Hashem: "Serve God with gladness; come before Him with joyous song."
Ki Mitzion: "For from Zion the Torah will come forth, and the word of God from Jerusalem."

Make fusion of endings and beginnings an occasion for Godly enchantment: Simchat Torah's ennobling cycle is here to inspire awe and spirit-augment.

* Helpful in crafting this Simchat Torah poem for 5776: "The Blessing of Moses" notes for Deuteronomy Chapter XXXIII, p. 909 in *Pentateuch and Haftorahs*, Dr. J.H. Hertz, Editor (Late Chief Rabbi of the British Empire); London, Soncino Press, 1999 and "Simchat Torah Songs" at Aish.com's Jewish Pathways website.

Simchat Torah in Liozna *

In Liozna near Vitebsk famished scholars in black frock coats and fox
fur-lined hats
Arrived at the ramshackle synagogue with its warped birch planks
While suffering from frostbitten fingers –
Yet numbness subsided when four maroon velvet Torahs
were lifted in a fiery frenzy,
And pious black-shod feet pranced at gazelles' speed
Around the regal navy velvet-draped reading table,
Circling seven transcendent times to honor God's female oversoul,
To celebrate seven faithful shepherd guests
Who graced soon-to-be-dismantled sukkah tabernacles.

The gangling, red-bearded sexton placed a lit silver candelabra
inside the now-empty ark
So that the Almighty's precious repository would not be eclipsed
by muddled darkness.
Ample blonde Rebbetzin Malke in her red wool dress led the other
women and their wide-eyed children
In an oval formation Torah triumph of gypsy-bright colors:
A forward-moving gavotte behind the whirling scrolls
with their jingling finials.

At midnight, the Liozna sexton found torn light-blue silk slippers and
broken beige satin heels
On the scuffed Gates of Fortitude sanctuary floor.
It is said that the Archangel Metat fashioned a noble crown for the Lord
From these tattered yet heavenly Simchat Torah festivity remnants.

* Inspired by two online Chabad.org essays with translation/adaptation by Yanki Tauber, from the writings of the sixth Lubavitcher Rebbe, Rabbi Yosef Yitzchak Schneersohn: "Hakafot in Liozna" and "A Crown of Slippers."

Chanukah: Festival of Jewish Singularity *

Stiff-necked scion of sand-trekker youth
Bore Hellenism's barbs but would not ban
Circumcision covenant, Sabbath, kashrut –
For ancient customs formed the Hebrew man.

Maccabees' bravura scotched a tyrant;
One blessed cruse let oil lamps glow for days –
The cult of Zeus made not one Jew compliant:
Our Temple Mount was meant for Godly ways.

Nine lights ablaze on blue-green menorah;
Zany orange dreidels, gold foil of coins
Filled with chocolate. Tawny latkes –
A vivid festival bright spirits join.

Feast of Lights: cauterized by conflict-past
Flares so much joy now freedom's won, at last!

* Inspired by the theme of Jewish singularity put forth in the "Hanukka: A Stiff-Necked People" chapter in Rabbi Adin Steinsaltz's book, *Change & Renewal: The Essence of the Jewish Holidays, Festivals & Days of Remembrance*, pp. 147-153 (Maggid Books, 2011).

The Dreidel Game

Start with twenty-six dreidels.
Sam will spin the large yellow dreidel with gold letters;
Abby will twirl the large orange dreidel with gold letters.
The small dreidels are see-through green, red, pink and blue,
Or wooden purple and turquoise painted hues.
"Let's play the dreidel game!" says Great-Aunt Barbara –
"It's the way to have fun before lighting Great-Grandma Sarah's
blue-green menorah."
Sam's big yellow dreidel falls on its side with "gimel" at the top –
"Gimme all those little dreidels!" he calls out, non-stop.
Abby's big orange dreidel shows "hey" after its spinning trip –
"Half the dreidels are mine now!" she calls out, and shakes her hips.
When Sam's dreidel lands on "nun" he can do nothing but let Abby
take a turn;
Then Abby's dreidel lands on "shin" so two little dreidels are handed
over to her brother, looking stern.

We'll play the dreidel game again in future Chanukah seasons,
For nun— gimel— hey— shin help teach us this holiday's amazing reasons.

Chanukah Villanelle

(Inspired by Rabbi Jonathan Sacks's essay, "8 Short Thoughts for 8 Chanukah Nights")

Bow not to Zeus Olympus in Temple sanctum!
Await Maccabee victories and cleansed oil;
Raise up menorah-beacon; be no longer glum!

One cruse amidst the wreckage was the holy sum:
Enough to rededicate faith's fortress soiled.
Bow not to Zeus Olympus in Temple sanctum!

Renew Hebrew prayers: chant, response, cry and hum;
Hasmonean purity tyranny did foil –
Raise up menorah-beacon; be no longer glum!

Band of few with spirit-strength crushed despot's thumb:
Mere arrows and shields nixed Antiochus turmoil.
Bow not to Zeus Olympus in Temple sanctum!

Jews' everlasting lights left Greek tragic heroes numb;
Beauty must wrap around one loving God's tight coil.
Raise up menorah-beacon; be no longer glum!

Set eight candle wicks ablaze — signs of hope to come;
Inner light, too, when shared reflects our Godly toil.
Bow not to Zeus Olympus in Temple sanctum!
Raise up menorah-beacon; be no longer glum!

Chanukah Reflection *

As the forlorn winter solstice approaches,
Light a carved jade lotus menorah in the Gobi Desert;
Strike a match to jasmine-scented candles
On an ivory elephant hanukkiyah while sailing over
An Indian Ocean once plied by Sephardic jewel merchants
Such as Maimonides' handsome, turbaned older brother.
Watch Ethiopians descended from Sheba and King David's author-son
Illuminate nine tapers on a golden African mask-motif candelabra
In the Gondar Compound Operation Solomon airlift refuge
Of skull caps, phylacteries and prayer shawls against nut-brown skin.

Remember Syrian-Hellenists' armored pachyderms,
swords and poisoned arrows;
Honor outnumbered Hasmonean Hebrew Herculean brothers
Who darted, scrambled, hunted, rearmed
To redeem the perpetual light of monotheism's purest olive oil.

Recall Bezalel's seven battered, ramrod-straight precious metal branches
Of a Temple Menorah that could only be brought to life
By Kohenim priests reaching with lamplighter poles from holy pavement.
Now *all* may set a blue-green Chanukah Menorah
with rainbow-hued tallow
Ablaze on a ledge framed by the tied gingham curtains
of the kitchen window;
All may place a silver candelabrum with tall lavender glims
on a parlor table
To greet and cheer weary Uncle Irving and Aunt Rachel after their
New England journey.

The Feast of Lights:
Time for sipping heated apple cider with cinnamon sticks
After accomplishing a democratic kindling.

* Inspired and informed by three online Chabad.org essays: "The Street-Lamp Lighter" and "A Little Band of Hasmoneans" by Rabbi Menachem M. Schneerson; "Chanukah Forever: The Infinite Leak" by Rabbi Tzvi Freeman.

Tu B' Shevat: Fruit of Redemption *

Unleash fruit tree sap of Shevat;
Let it run like an internal milk-of-life rivulet
Bound to awaken almond, fig, date, olive, pomegranate and carob pod
To promise springtime tithing of rainbow-hued produce
for cornucopia of nourishment
Provided to Levites, orphans and needy widows
By Providence-sparked farmers and their Jerusalem-bound oxen
All festooned with purple-twined bulrush baskets.

Partake of the apple of desire on the New Year of Trees,
Uttering a blessing pleasing to Israel's velvet-souled Almighty –
An arbor benediction overflowing like amphorae
spilling out amber palm honey.
Or speak of the grace of floral forgiveness presented as ambrosia
spooned from stone jugs
To satiate the silent, famished stranger's forbearing belly.
Such consecrations will hold enough sweetness
to coat Adam and Eve's transgression in Eden
With a Lordly, transcendent balm of myrrh, aloes and cinnamon –
And God in his munificence will not forget to furnish
An orange blossom pallet for celestial embrace.

* Inspired by two Chabad.org online essays: "15 Shevat: Blossoms in
the Winter?" by Rabbi Shlomo Yaffe and "Celebrating Pleasure, Tu B'
Shvat: A Mystical Interpretation" by Rabbi David Aaron.

Under God's Sacred Canopy *

Mid-winter in Northern climes has reduced tree branches to Shake-
speare's forlorn epithet:
"Bare ruined choirs."
But Holy Land trees now feel onset of springtime,
With running life-sap and moistened roots of heritage astir.

Kermes oaks on Mount Hermon have broad, Samson-strong trunks –
And mark the spot where the Lord promised Abraham land-inheritor
descendants of star sparkle.
The black mulberry on Mount Meron bears fruit as tasty as manna –
And owes its two-century vitality to planter-printer-farmer Rabbi Yis-
roel Beck of dreamy, whitewashed Safed.
The potent olive tree at Ein al-Asad has a glorious span of twenty-three feet:
Ideal for shade-seekers intent on absorbing high speech of prophets
dressed in humble garb.
Behold the peacemaker pistachio in Beit Netofa Valley –
How eagerly it has embraced former antagonists
for a diplomatic century and a half!
A hoary, tangled sycamore in Netanya is peekaboo host for scrambling
tots in red, blue, yellow and green play outfits;
A lemon-scented eucalyptus gum with its smooth yellow trunk towers
over the pious sharing Sabbath meals in low pastel apartment buildings
on a Petach Tikva street;
A Negev Desert acacia is an oasis-like haven for bicyclist picnickers and
hungry deer alike.
Doum date palms of the Arava Valley north of Eilat are lofty and slender–
With trunks divided in graceful twos
just like their East African river brethren.
Outstanding arbor of the Holy Land

does more than spew forth divine oxygen,

Glowing a dappled emerald green in intensifying sunlight:

Each wondrous tree in God's homeland instructs as it provides comforting shelter and refreshment.

Rejoice in Israel's awakening Sacred Canopy this mid-January Tu B'Shevat,

For another fortuitous, blessed and pristine New Year of Trees

Has achieved its resplendent primordial spread in our sphere.

* This poem for Tu B'Shevat was informed by Abigail Klein Leichman's online article, "The Top 10 Most Amazing Trees in Israel" (posted 3/13/13).

The title "Under God's Sacred Canopy" reflects the phrase Rabbi Harold Swiss of The Little Synagogue used in concluding his tender-hearted sermons.

Purim Shpiel: Delight of Triumph

Purim shpiel! Purim shpiel!
Adults perform the story of our people's salvation in Shushan:
Who will be comely Queen Esther?
A slender, intelligent, noble woman of the congregation is cast in the
people-savior role.
How shall we find forceful King Achashverosh?
Beauteous Esther's royal spouse shall be the top-ranking, charming, vibrant
raconteur-rabbi.
Who is worthy of portraying wise, patient and pious Uncle Mordechai?
This gray-haired sage incapable of bowing down to a statue-idol in a
procession can be a lay elder –
He who crafts soulful sermons from Grand Central Station encounters.
And the villain Haman of anti-Semitic infamy?
A congenial fellow with thespian flare will grumble and glare.

Purim shpiel! Purim shpiel!
Children celebrate the story of our people's salvation in Shushan:
See little boys flash aluminum swords as their scepters of acceptance;
Behold girlish curls, curtsies and purple velvet frocks
Bewitching enough to beguile the most imperious lord and master.
Follow sanctuary parade of youngsters twirling a cacophony of noisemakers:
Yellow harlequin mask groggers rattle Esther's veiled goodness;
Pink-and-black groggers grunt the perfidy of Haman.
Savor three-cornered Haman's haberdashery hamentashen,
With fillings of poppy, prune, apricot or raspberry:
They have the sweet taste of brotherhood, respect, tradition and refuge.
Rejoice as Mordechai the preteen on rocking horse surveys Persian citizens
From his uplifted vantage point of spiritual grandeur.

Purim shpiel! Purim shpiel!
Cherish and bequeath the story of our people's triumph in Shushan,
Passed on from generation to generation until Messiah's balm cures all
annihilation-trauma woes.

Purim shpiel! Purim shpiel!
Megillah scroll of Hebrew courage and virtue
is mirrored in its playful mimicry;
Sapphire and ruby of king and queen in sublime,
heartfelt bond it does convey.

No More Hamans!

An Amalekite descendant who brazenly nipped at the heels of the weak:

Haman! Haman! We gladly bid you adieu.

A traitorous, treacherous plotter whose schemes soared to heights of the gallows he built with bigotry's heat:

Haman! Haman! Truly gone? Don't expect boohoos.

An intolerant villain hoisted on his own petard due to hardened-heart misperceptions that almost obliterated Eden:

Haman! Haman! God scowls on such as you.

A moral miscreant whose twisted being was undeserving of the delicious taste of hamentashen — 'twas a crime to feed him:

Haman! Haman! Too bad you ever wooed!

An enemy of radiant Queen Esther and dear Uncle Mordechai—a viper-foe bringing venom to the purple-gold palace of King Achashverosh the Great:

Haman! Haman! Misogyny and misanthropy you were rightly taught to rue.

A pernicious Satan-soul is God-vanquished,

ever extinguishing his malicious preaching of hate:

Haman! Haman! The world has compassion and grace in your lieu.

Purim: Masks Donned and Removed

Esther!
Don the mask of a ravishing pagan regent obsessed with cosmetics and perfumes.
Remove that mask!
Reveal a beauteous daughter of Mosaic Covenant eager to deny herself peas and barley,
Then bravely battle a golden, lapis-encrusted scepter.

Mordechai!
Don the mask of a chattering elder too lazy to leave his comfortable encampment at the city gate.
Remove that mask!
Reveal comely Queen Esther's clever uncle capable of exposing all treachery at court,
Of hoisting the ignoble Haman the Amalekite on his own petard,
And bolstering a lioness niece in her effort to cushion her people
In purple silks of salvation.

Achoshverosh!
Don the mask of a wine-imbibing tyrant delegating power
To mediocre Haman: barber, bath attendant, social climber.
You were willing to dismiss Queen Vashti because she wouldn't dance
Sans her beloved pink veils, silver bustier and green harem pants;
Your focus was on gleaming treasury coffers rather than emerald justice.
Remove that mask!
Reveal a potentate capable of cherishing his virtuous Jewish regal mate and her ruby people,
Who has a towering gallows built for their foe:
Scheming, bigoted Haman and the sniping Haman clan.

A newly-enlightened sovereign sees righteous subjects as a cascade of onyx wealth!

Haman!
Don the mask of an upstanding, protective vizier whose wisdom and loyalty
Are like diamonds adorning the crown of his monarch –
The great pearl of Persia.
Remove that mask!
Reveal Haman the scoundrel who would misdirect power,
Leading to a possible scapegoat-bloodbath of innocents smitten for honest differences.
Haman the roguish, ice-hearted manipulator crushing sapphire goodness under his satanic stride;
Haman the twisted wildebeest stomping on topaz gentleness!
Haman the short-sighted crony trying to pulverize divine tiger's eye intention!
Villainous Haman each year defeated by wondrous moonstones and opals
Fastened by the Almighty on finials of the sublime, triumphant Purim Megillah scroll.

* Figurative masks in the Purim story are expounded on by Rabbi Adin Steinsaltz in the "Purim" chapter of his book *Change & Renewal: The Essence of the Jewish Holidays, Festivals and Days of Remembrance* (pp. 167-204); Maggid Books, Jerusalem, 2011.

Purim: Joy of Divine Unmasking

Boys don purple robes — garb of Persian king;
Girls in crimson sheaths: Queen Esther's mystery.
Beauty queen brought justice, life, liberty –
Adar is the month: salvation in the spring!

Sweet poppy paste in triangle dough — Haman's
Dastardly haberdashery bit, with hugs:
Heroine, villain blur with long sherry chugs –
Evil vizier triumphed *not* in Shushan!

Mordechai stood cedar-straight at palace gate:
Haman couldn't bend Israel's Lordly fold –
Loyal uncle rode Haman's steed (switch of fate):
A Hebrew man like lofty priests of old!

Haman drew lots: Persian eclipse, Judenrein –
Hashem doffed his carnival mask in time!

Purim Pantoum: Esther's Request *

A thousand years after Sinai's Covenant
Jews of Shushan clung to Moses' teachings
Though wicked viceroy Haman made them targets
Of Persian ire against Commandment folk.

Jews of Shushan clung to Moses' teachings
Eating kosher at king's banquet with no fear
Of Persian ire against Commandment folk.
Thoughts of lost First Temple: drowned with red wine!

Eating kosher at king's banquet with no fear
Folk could not foresee Queen Esther's three-day fast.
Thoughts of lost First Temple: drowned with red wine!
Toast fight-back decree — Semitic queen's request.

Folk could not foresee Queen Esther's three-day fast
Though wicked viceroy Haman made them targets.
Toast fight-back decree — Semitic queen's request
A thousand years after Sinai's Covenant.

* Informed and inspired by two Chabad.org online Purim essays
adapted by Yanki Tauber from the writings of the Lubavitcher Rebbe,
Rabbi Menachem Mendel Schneerson: "A Feast and a Fast" and "The
Thousand Year Difference."

Passover Libation *

First, drink a golden goblet of Agua Dulce Cabernet Sauvignon 2010
— dark, fruity Sierra Pelona Valley siren;
Then, toast God's opening expression of liberation meant for Moses
our shepherd of forbearance:
V'Hotzesi!
"I will take you out of Egypt!"
Next, imbibe a graceful champagne glass full of Alta Delta Chardonnay
2011 — greenish-white Casablanca temptress:
V'Hitzalti!
"I will deliver you from slavery!"
After that, down a slender frosted flute of Baron Herzog Merlot 2012
— that spicy, sassy, ruby red Central Coast bewitcher:
V'Goalti!
"I will redeem you!"
Finally, consume a snifter of Baron Edmund de Rothschild's Carmel
Moscato di Carmel 2013 — clear, sweet Holy Land charmer:
V'Lokachti!
"I will take you for a people!"

Do not forget to pour a silver chalice of lilac-pink Galil Mountain Rosé
2014 to gaze at in reverence:
This pristine fifth cup is for the elusive prophet Eliyahu -
Eagerly awaited Messiah's noble herald.
Open all portals and hear how Eliyahu channels the Lord's message of
ultimate Passover deliverance:
V'HeVeisi!
"I will bring you into the land which I promised your forefathers!"

Raise a "Hallelujah!" glass to chained agony of forced diaspora now undone.

* The Hebrew outcries of freedom associated with each cup of wine poured at the Passover Seder table are put forth by Rabbi Matis Blum in his book *Torah L'Daas*, and cited online in the essay "A Short Vort (or Two…or Three…) for Pesach" at haemtza.blogspot.com.

Pesach, Matzoh, MAROR! *

Search for stray breadcrumbs with a white feather in springtime –
For it is time to remember Moses' princely allegiance to Amram and Jocheved,
Hebrew parents who braved death to express marital love despite Pharoah's evil decree:
Pesach, Matzoh, Maror!
Buy an embroidered gold and beige satin matzoh covering –
Unleavened cracker-cakes will be displayed with dignity deserving of the bread of redemption;
Affliction-bread is an eternal reminder of the Mitzrayim-to-Canaan transition via Reed Sea, Lord's breath chasm:
Pesach, Matzoh, Maror!
Forget not flow of blood, sweat and tears while gleaning for straw to make baked mud bricks under relentless North African sun –
An inferno-crucible grilling bent backs as they stooped to cursing taskmasters cracking whips of inhumanity.
How ungodly the slaps that smote their noble cheeks when the strong dared pause to help the weak!
Pesach, Matzoh, Maror!

The bitter herb "maror" represents abuse endured as slaves;
It is a taste of humility well-known to stranger, orphan, widow –
As well as many a starving Sage!
Maror makes a honeyed Jewish soul thrive on kindness
to buffeted mortal brethren;
It is an empathy-engine that softens hearts in which gentleness reigns as king and queen.
Which Passover obligation most pleases God intent
on a Jew's salvation through

Righteous sensitivity as delicate as a butterfly's fluttering wings?
Maror, Maror, Maror!

* Pesach, matzoh and maror as three Passover obligations, and the primacy of maror (bitter herbs) in winning redemption for the Jewish people are put forth by Rabbi Matis Blum in his book *Torah L'Daas* — and posted by Harry Maryles online at haemtza.blogspot.com.

Passover: Let the Unfettering Begin! *

In the land of Horus's orange sunrises, narrow straits,
bull-worship and flavorful leeks
Pass over the sheep's blood-stained lintels
Of a simple, linen-clad shepherd people whose hoary, flashing Almighty
Wishes to preserve each feisty Hebrew firstborn
So that one day descendants will number as myriad grains of fine sand or
Be counted as stars in an infinitely-studded firmament.
Send out a strapping, golden-sandalled prophet-teacher from his arid
Midian refuge to pastures of Goshen;
Then have him plead with a tin-eyed, armor-hearted Pharaoh:
A despot brazen and twisted enough to imagine his own snake-soul self-
creation as a sublime emanation.
Let Miriam supervise swift baking of flat bread whose innocence
Almost persuaded the Lord to restore apple blossom-scented Eden.
Have Moses plant his copper Rameses court staff in parted Red Sea waters,
With reeds and coral levitating above like a bridal canopy,
Allowing tribe and mixed multitude
to pass underneath as kissing Cherubim –
Sans dignity-pinching bronze fetters worn
at the bleak storage city of Pithom.
Encourage soprano chanting of the Song of the Sea, joyous ululation,
leaping, prancing with timbrels
For seven sand-blown weeks in the season of buds
Until epiphany of eternal oasis-emancipation:
God's thunderous, supernal gift of scalloped granite Tablets of the Law–
Ten Utterances that would erect ladders
nearly reaching the sapphire heavens,
And someday make hallowed, emerald Galilean hills skip and frolic.

* This Passover poem was informed by the "Pesch" chapter in Rabbi Adin Steinsaltz's book *Change & Renewal: The Essence of the Jewish Holidays, Festivals & Days of Remembrance*, pp. 207 — 273; Maggid Books, Jerusalem, 2011.

Passover Bouquet *

Stack three round cakes — bread of indigence divine:
Gone, Egypt's golden bull debauchery!
Imbibe four silver goblets of blush wine:
Welcome, Sinai Desert sanctuary!
Bread of Affliction had freedom's savor;
Honey-manna coaxed smiles from bent ones.
Fruit of the vine brought bondage-release flavor,
For He would save, liberate, take Levite sons.
Watch Miriam vault, bound, leap on Reed Sea bank
With trills and tapping to please Almighty's soul.
See Moses' court staff plunge forward: leader's rank
Given to veiled gem in bosom-role.
Matzoh, wine, Sinai, Miriam, Moses:
Pesach in spring — Lord's gift of reddest roses!

* Informed and inspired by three Chabad.org online Passover essays based on the writings of the Lubavitcher Rebbe, Rabbi Menachem Mendel Schneerson: "The Matzot and Four Cups of Wine," "Vaulting, Bounding and Leaping" and "The Four Factions."

Anticipating Shavuot

For forty-nine nights — beginning with the second Passover Seder –
Remember how barley sheaves were waved,
Tied with hyssop-dyed violet cords,
Collected in gilded baskets –
Then presented to solemn Kohenim priests and eager Levite assistants
In their noble Jerusalem Temple sanctuary.
Stand straight as a cedar while reciting the blessing for each day's Omer
grain offering;
Conclude with a messianic wish:
"O Compassionate one! May He return for us
The Service of the Temple to its Place
Speedily and in our time. Amen; Selah." *

The forty-ninth eve is "Leil Shavuot":
The night before joyous acceptance of Torah and Ten Commandments
At a desert mount bathed in African heat and emanating tiger's eye beauty.
Commemorate this ancient turning point by studying, studying, studying–
With respected partner, cherished student, dear teacher.
Peruse texts of compelling Torah or order-seeking Talmud,
As did Rabbi Shimon bar Yochai of cave, carob tree, severe Roman con-
quest and dazzling Zohar fame,
Or Rav Yosef Karo of Spain, Turkey and Tzfat –
Whose *Shulchan Aruch* was a "Stone of Help" and "Breastplate of Judgment"
For those seeking a Jewish guidepost of pure white marble
Leading the way to a holy life in all circumstances. **

Morning kiddush to rejuvenate all-night scholars
Will be a display of dairy products overflowing with motherly nurture:
Ashkenazic cheesecake, cheese blintzes, cheese kreplach;

Syrian cheese sambusak, kelsonnes, atayef;
Iraqi sweet, buttery kahee dough;
Tunisian and Moroccan "siete cielos" seven-layer cake.

Such a lactic array would have pleased King Solomon,
Who wrote of his uplifting Hebrew bound-by-God heritage:
"Like honey and milk, it lies under your tongue." ***

* The concluding Blessing of the Omer (grain offering) prayer was cited online by Orthodox Union staff in the essay, "Basic Laws of Sefirat HaOmer" (www.ou.org/holidays/sefirat-haomer).

** The tradition of "Leil Shavuot" study sessions the night before the holiday begins is explained online by Rabbi Jack Abramowitz in his essay, "Shavuot: The All-Nighter" (www.ou.orea/holidays/shavuot).

*** Reasons for consumption of dairy products on Shavuot, and holiday dairy recipes of Jews from different parts of the world, are put forth in the "Dairy Foods" section of Wikipedia.org's essay on "Shavuot."

Shavuot: Pesach Perfected *

Count forty-nine days after Pesach freedom festival of Exodus-exaltation
For barley grain offering in crimson-threaded baskets
Given to chanting Temple priests by bowing, linen-clad farmers
Converging on Jerusalem from Galilee breadbasket or Valley of Jezreel.
On the fiftieth day, kiss pea-green Holy Land fields and tawny desert dunes
In gratitude for gift of Sinaitic Torah given in unleavened haste
To semi-liberated, booth-dwelling wanderers in search of a post-Reed-
Sea-crossing era
Of Law, commandment, stricture, example:
A peoplehood-congregation chose to do, hear, say according to
Almighty's argent image mounted on a sapphire chariot-throne.

It is Shavuot –
Late springtime season for reverencing
Prophet, intercessor, pleader, mediator, teacher, holy scribe
Moses who cradled Scalloped Tablets with heavenly chiseled Ten Ut-
terances
Meant to serve as a stone fence to shepherd in kine with a tendency to
stray from Lordly intention.
The Law by Him conceived, by an amethyst nation embraced:
An ever-turning vellum scroll with Tree-of-Life ken enlaced.

* The connection between Pesach (Passover) and Shavuot (Festival of
Weeks) is put forth by Rabbi Adin Steinsaltz in the "Shavuot" section
of his book *Change & Renewal: The Essence of the Jewish Holidays, Festivals
& Days of Remembrance*, pp.295-333; Maggid Books, Jerusalem, 2011.

Shavuot: Celestial Breakthrough *

An emerald-eyed seraph in green cloak
Tried to snatch the Scroll Moses cradled in mist.
The shepherd defended his Master's bequest:
"Do cherubs covet, or use Sabbath yokes?
Sandy feet beneath the Holy Mount need
Torah's nudge to date-palm-oasis path."
God and prophet straddled heaven and earth
As though galloping on vertical white steeds.
Lightning landings, thunder-boom intonings:
Ten Demands to bolster cracked stone walls
Seeking fine masonry to repair flaws.
This drama preceded a desert greening:
The Amber Hill sprouted forsythia bells!
Next dawn, ibex milk was served from clay stores.

* Informed and inspired by two Chabad.org online Shavuot essays based on the writings of the Lubavitcher Rebbe, Rabbi Menachem Mendel Schneerson: "Real Estate" and "The Breakthrough."

Batsheva's Kinot *

Lord, why do You allow your people to be accused of blood libel's blasphemous ignominy?
Well You know that Your Chosen Ones are forbidden to sever the limb
of a living animal,
May not drink blood or create the food abomination "blood sausage",
Cannot eat kosher unless sprinklings of snow-white crystals
Have caused encarnadine liquid to drain off poultry.
Let it be known that Your blood-soaked warriors eschew carnage –
Fighting only when nursing mothers, children in Torah academies,
Roses of sharon, lilies of the field, red anemones,
Date palms and red prickly pear cacti
Know not blessings of shalom.

Lord, why must Your scattered devotees be persecuted for love of Zion?
In France Almighty's doorpost mezuzah, pious blue knitted skullcap,
gold Star of David pendant –
Emblems of the ancient faith of Moses and Sinai Revelation –
Serve as a Daniel-in-the-lion's den temptations
for beatings and fire bombings,
Even for kidnapping and immolation:
As the soul of the falsely romanced young Parisian Ilan Halimi –
He of the handsome face and beatific smile –
Can eternally attest.
Dear Lord, restore a world where Your mezuzah,
Lord Is One prayer people
Need not fear to display the Hebrew letter
"shin" for "Shaddai" the Almighty,
Because all will apprehend it as the pure-hearted declaration of
Monotheism's aged matriarch-creator

Who whispers the "Ten Commandments" into the ears of gentle newborns
From generation to generation,
In Zion and Diaspora alike.

Lord, why do you tolerate insidious canker of "moral equivalency"?
The Metropolitan Opera schedules "The Death of Klinghoffer" –
But the wheelchair-ridden Jewish appliance manufacturer shot in head
and chest on an anniversary cruise
Is hardly portrayed as the unequivocal tenor-hero.

IDF soldiers enter the Gazan hornet's nest only after rockets reach Tel
Aviv, Jerusalem and Haifa.
Hamas's "human shield" tactics are minimized
While charges of "Nazism" and "genocide"
are unleashed against the defending state.
Lord, make clear the parameters of courage and justice
Sanctioned by Your all-knowing wisdom;
Help us forge a path cleared of thistles and brambles that scrape,
Planted with fragrant cedars
providing life-affirming shade from relentless heat –
A byway of moral clarity ripe for shalom/salaam.

* Kinot — Poetic prayer-dirges recited on Tisha B'Av, the Jewish day
of mourning, for calamities such as the destruction of the two ancient
Jerusalem Temples, Spanish Inquisition and Warsaw Ghetto deporta-
tion, which occurred during summer months. The "kinot" tradition
started with the prophet Jeremiah's Book of Lamentations, set during
the harsh Babylonian siege of Jerusalem, 6th Century B.C.E. "Kinot"
traditionally implore God regarding cruelties that others have inflicted
on the Jewish people.

"Batsheva's Kinot" were informed by events of Summer 2014, and a reading of "A Sample of Kinot and their Translations for Consecutive Reading on Tisha B'Av" by A. Katz, retrieved from beureihatefila@yahoo.com (copyright 2008). Also consulted: "The Shocking Murder of Ilan Halimi" by Deborah Freund, retrieved from Aish.com.

Day after Tisha B'Av, 5774

Only One-Day Tisha B'Avs: Sight, Hearing, Voice Recovered

Avert eyes! Cover ears!

A noble California Redwood is felled;

A purposeful shattering of carved stone mountain Buddha in Afghanistan is executed;

Chattel abductions of sailor-slaves in South-East Asia are happening now.

Eyes can be selectively directed to watching lemon-yellow forsythia bell blooms in April;

Ears can be trained to listen intently to baritone sighs of Mahler's Lied "I am Lost to the World."

But ancient Kohanim priests did not cover eyes or ears

As Jerusalem stone walls of rainbow limestone caved in

After breaches by Nebuchadnezzar and Vespasian's troops lumbering forward like famished bears,

Flashing hand axes and pushing siege towers to ensure rivers of blood and hunger-thirst scourges.

Sight, hearing, smell, touch were deployed as torch fires consumed purple-blue curtains

Of the Holy of Holies, and Solomon's choice Lebanon cedar timbers crashed with Apocalyptic force.

Men of fervent faith chanted Psalms of David and "Hear, O Israel!" with impassioned discipline,

Palms outstretched to accompany the Priestly Blessing for grace of

God's shining, smiling Countenance bestowed as Shepherd of all Israel.

Then sight, hearing, voice turned to ash.

Abject Hebrew slaves were taken to Babylon, to Rome.

Zion was an ever-chased orphan;

Foxes ran through the forlorn Temple Courts.

Uncover eyes and ears!
Unleash a choir of rumbling voices!
Zion no longer suffers Tisha B'Av lamentation daily through the beleaguered epochs.
Kohanim may assemble at the Western Wall for shachrit, mincha and ma'ariv prayers
Reading from Holy Tongue siddurim, and inquiring about wives and children
In the miracle of Modern Hebrew's musical, guttural cadence.
Kibbutzniks run guest houses with views of the tranquil Sea of Galilee and Beguiling Dead Sea — a treasure-trove basin of minerals.
Artists sell paintings of lively Tel Aviv bounded by a turquoise Mediterranean,
Of eons-old Jerusalem with walls, turrets, domes, steps.
Mystics seek refuge in hilly Galilean Safad's cool, white-washed synagogues,
Or in Judean and Negev Deserts with their purifying crucible of moon landscape rock-and-dune formations.
Ethiopian, Russian and French new immigrants renew hope,
Having found a kaleidoscope haven in the Levant.

Tisha B'Av summer commemoration of shackled, beaten-down catastrophe
Lasts but one day — and not every day—
In the Zion-redeemed Mosaic psyche.

Tisha B'Av: Sorrow in Summer *

There is an "All Sorrows Day"
Set aside for mourning while seated on low stools,
For chanting Jeremiah's dirges of siege, heat, hunger and thirst,
For remembering chink of Roman chains and shame
of Temple Menorah become plunder.
It is a fair summer day of fullness and warmth,
Belied by base human actions beginning two-and-a-half millennia ago–
Perpetrated in that otherwise idyllic season of tendrils and roses.

Judah's palms blessed the blood trickling down portico steps
Flowing from forever stilled, prostrate bodies of Temple priests
On two calamitous occasions.
Spain's jasmine wept as physicians, astronomers, philosophers, poets
and pregnant beauties
Marched, marched, marched from parched towns to azure coast
For expulsion-rescue on Turkish sailing ships.
Germany's firs bowed down in reverence
As cattle cars with tender souls of the Mosaic flock
Hurtled toward eastern hinterlands of personhood-trampling oblivion.

In sultry weather, conquer melancholy
By invoking Joshua and Caleb's confidence as Holy Land surveyors;
Levite Temple foot-bathing-with-pitcher routines of loving discipline;
Kohanim all-night vigils at three stations of Temple and Mount
As reflections of the charitable Godly life.

For every forced diaspora and pogrom,
Rub balm of Gilead on mind's scars –

Then soak up sun on bench by vine and fig tree,
Triumphing over dire summer setbacks.

* Informed, in part, by the United with Israel online essay, "Where is the Holy Temple? Are We Still Living with the Biblical Spies?" and the Chabad.org online essay, "Tisha B'Av and the 3 Weeks: The Temple Guards and Their Mystical Meaning."

II. IN A PIOUS MOOD

Priestly Raiment*

(Inspired by Parsha Tetzaveh: Exodus 27:20 — 30:10)

Remake Joseph's cloak of violet, crimson and turquoise wool:
Aaron as Kohen Gadol will ask the Lord's forgiveness
For crimes of abandonment, abduction and untruth.

Stitch white linen pants of modesty to cover loin and legs:
May the priestly petition for fidelity, prudence and reverence
Be fulfilled by a people chosen for a pure pearl lifestyle.

Fashion a robe with pomegranate-shaped silver bells
sewn to the bottom hem:
Pleasant chimes heard when God's emissary moves are a warning –
Beware the cacophony of clattering chatter that degrades these three:
One who speaks, one who hears, one who is spoken about.

Don the tall miter with its heavenward peak:
Repent for Tower of Babel arrogance,
For haughty assumptions of perfection
by flawed sons and daughters of Cain.

Jeweled breastplate of onyx and gold banishes tarnished judgments that
are disingenuous;
Gold forehead plate is a cerebral crown pleading for discipline of care-
ful consideration;
An apron adds a layer of extra protection against pitfall of idolatry's in-
famous pull;
Trunk sash girds the devout heart
so that there is no room for sultry daydreaming

When trembling prayer is offered to the one Master of Creation.

Wool in rainbow stripes, fine linen, gleaming silver, gold, beckoning gemstones:
Such royal raiment for the respected Hebrew priestly clan!
Outside the Tabernacle?
Inner beauty was the vestment of choice
Worn by each Israelite child, woman and man.

* "Priestly Raiment" is informed by the Aish.com online essay "Tetzaveh: Symbolic Clothes" by Rabbi Abba Wagensberg and by Rabbi Jill Hausman's "Sabbath Week: Shabbat Tetzaveh" column entitled "The Essence of Jewish Royalty" in *The Jewish Week* (2/7/14, p. 57).

After Candle-Lighting Prayer

May the children, grandchildren and great-grandchildren
in this family practice "tikkun olam" –
Making the world a Godly sapphire refuge as they strive to serve in goodness.
Please bring peace/shalom/salaam to every corner of the globe –
Guiding diplomats to rise above stormy outlooks so that they become
towering statesmen,
Nudging everyday people to uncover the purple treasure of shared humanity.

Help heal the Earth:
Let land's emerald crown, water's blueness and a crystal clear troposphere
Ever sustain the Creation You so lovingly crafted in six symbol-clashing days.

Watch over all who struggle to walk the path of gleaming righteousness
in ruby rectitude,
Knowing that the very young and very old need extra protection under
Your ebony powerhouse wings.

Dear Almighty,
Consider this fervent after candle-lighting prayer
As Your rainbow-pearl assignment
For this wondrous Shabbat.

Prayer for Peace in the Levant

Oh God!
In lands of camel caravan, arid desert moonscape,
blessed oasis charm, lush palm groves;
Where olives, pita, falafel, tahina, hummus, tabouleh, couscous, dates
and honey
Grace tables of poor and prosperous alike;
Where humble donkeys with modest riders clatter along ancient cobblestones;
Where gentle shepherds watch over sheep descended from Moses' herds–
We beg of You the wisdom, statesmanship and soaring mindfulness
Needed to achieve shalom/salaam for all Semites, Druze, Turks, Kurds,
Yazidis, Persians and Berbers
Who inhabit the Levant with its tiger's eye beauty
and Lion of Judah nobility.
Comfort Your goodly people of rectitude whose forbearance is angelic;
Rebuke all forces that instigate tyranny;
Break the cycle of travail that first made Jeremiah weep!

Hallelujah! Peace is Your balm of Gilead.
Selah! Healing is Your tender benediction.
Amen! Rebuilding will be Your Lordly consecration.
Dear God!
Hallelujah! Selah! Amen!

Divine Intervention

Lord, when I pray it is a granite bedrock effort:
Powerful because You will not buckle under the weight of my gray sorrows;
Hard because I am allowed no intermediaries to help countenance
The lava flow of Your volcanic will.

Personal petition is a fault line leaving me no recourse to hold steady
Using braided candle and silver spice box charms
as quake-quelling comforters –
Yet I am in the habit of sneaking in a wheelbarrow full of gravel
To patch up foibles of humanity and fix ruts marring Your sphere
By imploring you to dole out golden-nugget favors
from Your merciful female over-soul
After I have recited Hebrew Sabbath Bride benedictions over
Two blazing, bone-white tapers held in crystal candlesticks
on Fridays at prism-sunset –
A basalt-brave, nonagenarian mother at my side.

Lord, let my piety flow as forcefully as Iceland's geysers and Victoria's Falls,
Splashing the horizon of Firmament and Earth,
Connecting them with a rainbow-rung ladder
Of goodly tiger's eye, malachite and blue topaz intentions.

Transcendence

Aged weeping willows bow by the bay
Widows in black lace light candles at dusk
Copper beech at three-hundred: crown falls away.

Gift-giving sows remembrance's heart-sway
Embraces bestowed bundle forlorn husks
Aged weeping willows bow by the bay.

Kisses granted freely treatises say
Hoary temple bobbers exude sweet musk
Copper beech at three-hundred: crown falls away.

Kindness is eternity's gentle ray
Good deeds have force of an elephant's tusks
Aged weeping willows bow by the bay.

With seashells and stream rocks one's walk array
Speak in bell tones, cadence never brusque
Copper beech at three-hundred: crown falls away.

White shroud in plain pine box: not the final say
For souls that stroked a needy Earth in flux.
Aged weeping willows bow by the bay
Copper beech at three-hundred: crown falls away.

The Cloak of Faith

Shield of David, Torah breastplate and Kiddush cup goblet in gleaming silver:
The cloak of faith!
Kohen priest's white linen garment with pomegranate-shaped bells on
the hem to warn of purity's approach:
The cloak of faith!
Moses' granite Tablets of the Law, a rose marble Ark of the Covenant,
a pottery menorah with blue-green glaze:
The cloak of faith!
A gold "yad" pointer encrusted with rubies for a righteous one's read-
ings from the Holy Scroll:
The cloak of faith!
A flowing black-and-white striped prayer shawl stored in a crimson velvet
"tallith" bag with room for frayed, cherished brown leather phylactery:
The cloak of faith!
A devout, youthful Jewish couple who have brought their first son and
first daughter into a rumbling world that they will one day help to calm,
guide and perfect:
The cloak of faith!

Mighty Fifty *

Fifty days from the first Passover of unleavened Egyptian flight
To Torah Revelation at amber expanse before Sinai's Mount of modest height.

Fifty foaming orange mystical Levantine sunrises separated
Green leek-shoots of faith's tentative inception from honey-white Sabbath manna that sated.

Fifty eerie, starry indigo desert evenings
of bonfires and meandering encampment
Allowed Moses and Aaron to nudge stragglers
using acacia staffs, heaven-sent.

Seven weeks and one more morn is a time span
for wisdom, discipline, charity as reverie- preparation
For acceptance of Ten Commandment Tablets (beloved strictures
sculpted for a trail-blazing nation).

Cut and count handfuls of barley as Omer offerings cascading into
springtime bulrush baskets –
From nadir of slavery to Shavuot triumph shows growing spirit-bounty
of God's Pentecostal stint.

Fifty silver shekels from each tribal prince started lifting, hammering,
dyeing at Tent of Meeting — Lordly work;
Fifty golden loops secured awesome purple drapery enfolding Holy of
Holies and its Ark.
Fiftieth is Jubilee year of field reversion and Hebrew household servant
manumission:

Blow shofars from Temple turrets and Galilean hilltops to honor one mighty number's uplifting vision.

* Inspired and informed by the Chabad.org online essay, "Who Knows Fifty? The distinguished number of transcendence" by Osher Chaim Levene, with Rabbi Yehoshua Hartman (excerpted from the book *Jewish Wisdom in the Numbers*).

Post-Surgery Genuflection

(In gratitude to Dr. Howard Nadjari, North Shore Hospital surgeon
par excellence)

Courage, faith and medicine are among His tender mercies –
The syncopated heartbeat of an aged matriarch will yet conceive rhyth-
mic epiphanies!

Countless are the times He has stayed the hand of the Angel of Doom–
Let tears flow for the Master of Compassion who sees all, and must abide!

Pity is his arsenal when the vulnerable need bolstering –
Ponder the glorious scope of His discernment and penchant for reprieve!

Lord of Second Chances celebrates the strong and gently embraces the weak–
Intone grateful prayers for the marvel of unending miracles!

Bow down to He who inspired David's psalms –
Cry hallelujah three times daily as sustenance
for the hungry, yearning earth-soul!

The Holy Fabric

(Inspired by the "Sh'ma Now" column essays dealing with "Simcha —
Joy" that appeared in the May 20, 2016 *Forward*)

While night and day are stitched in patches,
Pain and cheerfulness serve as warp and weft;
Humdrum and holiday form bargello swatch,
Lull and drama twine in silver-gold heft –
Then God in heaven is pleased with His
Tapestry of contrasts with which the globe
Is draped. Cloth's embroidery's amiss
Sans couching with pride and shame on human robe.
Wool in hues of envy-green and lilac –
Confidence may turn disharmony to
Crocheted flower faces — spring's smiling stock;
Wary, fond: squares sewn for afghan throw.
Strange to find salvation in fabric's pull –
But tension's knit is beauty when soul's full.

Bardic Drumbeats

Tooth-toot, lip-press, throat-rumble, tongue-lull:
Sounds for clarion's clash or nursing's coo;
Sibilants for Eden-sin, secret love's rue –
Fireworks of lemon bursts; green apples hulled.

For soliloquy or lieder, heart's pull
Shrieks ruined peace, and corrupts flesh to dew.
A threnody of woe crept, rose, snuck, flew –
With lavish darker notes this globe is full.

Hear "tintinnabulations" wrung from Poe;
Grasp how death "thought, swelled, died": Donne's depth;
Weep for Keats' "haggard knight" in "elfin grot";
Know "Gitche" on "red crag quarry": Longfellow.
"Break, break, break!": stones of Tennyson's graceless lot –
Consonants are bardic drumbeats. Godly breadth!

III. RIGHTEOUS WARRIORS

Moses: Mission and Demise *

Gently place Tzipporah and Gershom on a holy, humble donkey;
Begin the trek from sands of Midian to forbidden fleshpots of Egypt.
Prepare to confront Pharaoh of the hideous, icy speech:
Almighty of Existence, Compassion, Justice, Forbearance
Demands liberation of famished, brick-laying slave-tribe with welts of woe–
For Israelites were meant to toil in freedom:
Open-flapped tents of prayerful convocation would shelter Hebrew laborers
Forging world-betterment.

Shepherd an earnest flock from plague-ridden, formerly fertile Nile
Across parted Reed Sea depths:
Grief for drowned chariot drivers and their muscular Arabian stallions
Would only allow songs of grateful joy with tapping timbrel
Once Sinai's dunes for meandering and Mount of Revelation
Appeared on the other side in a reassuring swath of
Orange-red horizon.

Plead for permission for entrance
to the Holy Land for Pharaoh's nemesis –
For that eternal, princely act surely would have eclipsed Diaspora
With its doleful return to shackled anonymity.
Wear ashes and sackcloth when the Lord of Hosts denies this poignant
plea for prophet and people.

Accept God's feathery farewell kiss while deep asleep in onyx darkness;
Let glorious images of nursing Yocheved, Nile-bathing Batya, musical Miriam,
Anguished Amram and harmonious High Priest Aharon
Pass through the light-emanating mind of an awesome Deity-confidant,
guide, teacher,

Heroic emissary for the ages and first Chief Rabbi
One last, lustrous time.

* Informed by Yanki Tauber's essays on the teachings of Rabbi Schneerson at Chabad.org: "Moses: The Birth of a Leader," "Moshiach's Donkey" and "I Am."

Brother Soldier *

My gentle brother has gone to war.
In his knapsack he carefully placed Psalms of David, the musical warrior king
And a verse volume by pacifist Independence fighter Yehuda Amichai.
His educated wife just gave birth to triplets:
Eyal, Gilad, Naftali.
When he adjusts the embedded lens that serves as
Slit lion eyes of an olive green Sabra Merkava "chariot" tank
He imagines the new mother nursing,
Singing tender lullabies in Hebrew, Yiddish and Ladino –
In the bomb shelter of a Jerusalem bookstore, if need be.
As he risks his Bible and Talmud-imbued being
To obliterate terror tunnels reinforced with concrete –
A mixture his native country sent over
for help with quotidian people projects–
He lives or dies for integrity of soil promised as a Holocaust refuge,
Where plague of incoming projectiles and incursions of lethal intent
Threaten to replace terrain of milk and honey with inferno of
Blaring fifteen-second warning sirens, safe room retreats, bomb shelter huddling,
Constant thwarting of kibbutz and beach massacres and abductions –
Even Ramat Gan Zoo elephants squeal and shoo their young,
Trying to shield them from man's inhumanity raining down from un-natural skies.

My gentle brother has gone to war.
May he return victorious to the echo of silver trumpets,
With the strength of Jonah's behemoth,
As sound of senses as Joshua,
As sound of limbs as Samson,

As articulate as Isaiah.
If he should come back only for a soulful embrace,
Let Zion take comfort in the memory of Moses' beatific smile
Before he led triumphant Israelites in battle against undermining Midianites–
Though he knew God had ordained that to be his last living conquest.

My gentle brother has gone to war.
May he trudge righteous footsteps of Father Abraham's unbent path
On this globe and in the World to Come.

* Written during Israel's Operation Protective Edge.

When the Righteous Were Outnumbered

At the Battle of Monmouth,
rows of King George's dutiful Redcoats plodded forward –
But crafty, outflanked Colonials used agile horse, hill high-ground,
reappearing cannon, relentless maneuver and alert command to show
them up as cowards.

Troops recruited from Jordan, Lebanon, Syria, Iraq, Egypt, Saudi Arabia and Yemen swooped down on the nascent Jewish State in 1948;
A million scrappy, impassioned European Holocaust and Arab-Jewish
refugees enlisted the help of Irish pilots, exploding seltzer bottles, Edward G. Robinson's Hollywood earnings for arms and limitless survivor-grit to sculpt a happier fate.

Eight-thousand afflicted with the dastardly retching-bleeding virus that
spread from African bush to towns and cities, in due course;
Only one-third of that total: number of Doctors Without Borders personnel fighting the scourge at its South-East Atlantic, sun-kissed lands source.

A thousand brazen, well-financed decapitation experts trying to take
Kobani on Turk-Syrian border;
Hundreds of valiant peshmerga fight-to-the-death-for-the-purpose-of-
life warrior men and women fed on bread and water.

Twelve soaring arias for "freedom fighter" terrorists who turned a couple's anniversary cruise into a Mediterranean hell on earth;
Alas: a mere five meager arias for devoted wife, and wheelchair-bound
Jewish manufacturer husband who dared respond before being shot and
flung into aqua depths, forever deprived of blessed turf!

When the righteous are outnumbered some clashes are won,
and some are lost:
God's tears formed this sphere's great waterfalls
for the precious lives so cost.

The Purple Badge of Merit *

It is balmy August, 1782 at Dutch-style Hasbrouck House
in Newburgh, New York.
His Excellency General Washington has one remaining task
Before the free, cold and hunger-tested patriots
of a victorious Continental Army
Could become farmers, teachers, candle makers, coopers, carriage mak-
ers, coachmen and bakers once again:
The heart-shaped purple silk Badge of Merit with silver lace trim on a
woolen backing –
Complete with crocheted white lettering –
Must be pinned over the left breast of officer or enlisted trudger
Whose gallantry, fidelity, meritorious action, bravery, good conduct
and wounding
By an instrument of war in the hands of a pernicious foe
Has proven his unexampled fortitude.

Sergeant Elijah Churchill:
Fourth Troop, Second Regiment of Light Dragoons.
Fort St. George on Long Island was a forage depot with tons of hay to
nourish British horses through the winter.
Destroyed in an inferno that would have made Dante proud!
Fort Slongo on Long Island's North Shore was jam-packed with enemy
supplies sorely needed by Continental soldiers –
Some of whom were boiling and eating their shoes.
Bounty captured!
Sergeant William Brown:
5th Connecticut Regiment attached
to Lieutenant Alexander Hamilton's troops.
The British inner defense line at Yorktown

Could only be overcome by initial action of bayonets as mute as church mice,
Then running deer-like with an Indian's grace,
Nimbly climbing trees with needle-sharp limbs
meant to impale as many Blue Coats
as possible in New World crucifixions,
Surviving a murderous ten-minute hail of musket fire
like a scene out of Hades.
Done!

Sergeant Daniel Bissell:
2nd Connecticut Regiment; spy –
Supposed deserter who joined Benedict Arnold's Corps of New York
City Loyalists.
No British troop movements in and around the Knickerbocker-Union
Jack-Stars and Stripes hybrid went unnoticed by Bissell –
Via notes, memoranda and memorization –
For burning of papers became necessary
when slow-as-molasses British intelligence
Finally discerned that sleeper agents lay in their midst
Like vipers ready to transport the venom of truth.
Each day could have ended in a gibbet –
Or a noose hung from an apple tree at East Broadway and Market Streets–
As it did for captured, Yale-educated schoolmaster-soldier-spy Nathan Hale
Who, denied minister and Bible,
crafted his own noble-as-a-dovish eagle parting prayer.
Instead, outwitting accomplished!

The first three candidates inscribed in the Book of Merit
Proudly wore the Purple Badge of those whose souls
Do battle like a Colossus unleashed.
Blood has gushed from the most lion-hearted protectors

of our homeland's native or adopted soil
Twenty-five thousand times since the founding cornerstone
marking this nation's birth.
Today's heroes and heroines whose Purple Emblem agility is wed to
sublime purpose
Face carnage and concussion as they erect scaffolding in exotic lands
To help uphold Jefferson's three-pronged framework
for American liberty's ideals.
May the Lord preserve the synapse-sinew-spirit triumvirate
that is their eternal glory!

* Purple Badge of Merit facts were gleaned from British-born West Point professor Ray Raymond's detailed and poignant essay, "The Badge of Military Merit." It can be found online at http://www.purple-heart.org/HistoryMedal2.aspx.

Memorial Day, 2014

I Shall Sing

Because toddlers smile and wave at strangers,
Although I am alone in the night
I shall sing.

Because an old veteran of the righteous war sells red cloth poppies
In front of the Chase Bank,
Although I am not a queen with beauty's crown in the morning
I shall sing.

Because gentle couples open the door to Barnes & Noble when they see
An old woman who loves to read,
I who walk the path of willows that cry
Beside bitter waters in the afternoon –
I, too, shall sing!

I shall sing because the trembling soul will return
To the nest of her Maker
Like a nightingale discovering lightness of air
Filled with gossamer angels that guide hopeful wings
To the Garden of Eden of Merciful Messiah:
All shall sing!

אַשִׁירָה

כִּי פָּעוֹטִים מְחַיְּכִים וּמְנוֹפְפִים לְזָרִים,
לַמְרוֹת שֶׁאֲנִי לְבַד בַּלַּיְלָה
אַשִׁירָה.

כִּי חַיָּל זָקֵן מֵהַמִּלְחָמָה הַמּוּצְדֶּקֶת מוֹכֵר פְּרָגִים עֲשׂוּיִים מִבַּד
בַּחֲזִית בַּנְק צֵ'ייס,
לַמְרוֹת שֶׁאֲנִי לֹא מַלְכָּה עִם כֶּתֶר יוֹפִי בַּבּוֹקֶר
אַשִׁירָה.

כִּי זוּגוֹת עֲדִינִים הַפּוֹתְחִים אֶת הַדֶּלֶת שֶׁל בָּארְנְס אֶנְד נוֹבְּל כַּאֲשֶׁר הֵם רוֹאִים
אִשָׁה זְקֵנָה שֶׁאוֹהֶבֶת לִקְרוֹא,
אֲנִי שֶׁהוֹלֶכֶת בִּשְׁבִיל הָעֲרָבוֹת הַבּוֹכִיּוֹת
עַל יַד מַיִם מָרִים אַחֲרֵי הַצָּהֳרַיִם-
גַּם אֲנִי אַשִׁירָה!

אַשִׁירָה כִּי הַנְּשָׁמָה הָרוֹעֶדֶת תַּחֲזוֹר
לְקֵן בּוֹרְאָהּ
כְּמוֹ זָמִיר מַצְוִי הַמְגַלֶּה אֶת קְלוּת הָאֲוִיר
הַמָּלֵא בְּמַלְאָכִים עִם כַּנְפֵי מַלְמְלָה דַּקִּיקָה הַמַּנְחִים כַּנְפֵי תִקְוָה
לְגַן עֵדֶן שֶׁל מָשִׁיחַ רַחֲמָן׃
כּוּלָם יָשִׁירוּ!

--בַּת שֶׁבַע הַנְטְמֶן

Five Earth-Angels

(Dedicated to the five precious souls who perished in the Har Nof Jerusalem Massacre of November 18, 2014: Rabbi Aryeh Kupinsky, Rabbi Moshe Twersky, Rabbi Avraham Shmuel Goldberg, Rabbi Kalman Levine and Police Officer Zidan Saif)

Four rabbis walking in rectitude;
A Druze policeman of character gallant and loyal:
One common destiny among things that clash –
Prayer books, prayer shawls, phylactories, Holy Ark,
meat cleavers, axes, guns
In the Congregation of the Children of the Hebrew Bible Scroll –
Next to a wooded West Jerusalem hill and charming limestone streets.
There were rivers of the blood of the righteous, pure and innocent
Instead of a peaceful sea of wisdom and goodness.
The rabbi with the Giant Og's height and Samson-strength
Shouted "Run!" to the other virtuous sages,
And stayed to throw crimson-streaked
devotionals, velvet chairs, long study tables –
Until wounds as deep as a chasm delivered him to his Maker.
Where was pity, clemency, sacred protection for the five earth-angels
That early November morning when gentleness and gentlemanliness
Were interrupted by barbarity of iceberg hearts?
The three-month-old baby boy of the bullet-riddled,
head-wounded Druze policeman
Whose coffin was draped with the blue Star of David;
The thoughtful grandchildren of the dignified rabbis:
These seeds of our future will seek solace someday
In the well-improved world
That we must promise to sculpt.

Los cinco ángeles de la tierra

(Dedicado a las cinco almas preciosas quienes perecieron en la matanza de Har Nof en Jerusalén, el 18 de noviembre del 2014: El rabino Aryeh Kupinsky, El rabino Moshe Twersky, El rabino Avraham Shmuel Goldberg, El rabino Kalman Levine y el policía Zidan Saif)

Cuatro rabinos caminando en rectitud;
Un policía druso de caracter valiente y leal:
Un destino común entre las cosas que chocan -
Los devocionarios, los mantones del rezo, las filacterias, el arca sagrada, los cuchillos de carnicero, las hachas, las pistolas
En Los Fieles de Los Hijos del Papiro del Biblio Judio –
Próximo a un monte arbolado en Jerusalén Oeste y las calles encantadoras de piedra caliza.
Eran ríos de sangre de los honrados, los puros y los inocentes
En lugar de un mar tranquilo de sabiduría y benevolencia.
El rabino con la estatura del gigante Og y la fuerza de Sansón gritó "¡Corran!" a los otros sabios
Y quedó para tirar los devocionarios rayados de carmesí, las sillas aterciopeladas y las mesas largas de estudio –
Hasta que las heridas tan profundas como un abismo le entregó a su Hacedor.
¿Dónde estaban la lástima, la clemencia, la protección santa para los cinco ángeles en la tierra
Esa madrugada de noviembre cuando la bondad y la caballerosidad
Eran interrumpidas por el barbarismo de corazones de icebergs?
El bebé de tres meses del policía druso lleno de heridas de balas en la cabeza
Cuyo ataúd era cubierto con la estrella azul de David;
Los nietos pensativos de los dignos rabinos:
Estas semillas de nuestro futuro buscarán el consuelo algún día

En un mundo muy mejorado
Que nosotros deberíamos prometer esculpir.

Israel at 67

Descendants of usurers have again become people of the fields!
Ashes of Holocaust's cultivated innocents have reassembled themselves
Into vibrant bones of IDF teens in the noble Golani Brigade –
And arise phoenix-like as profiles of disciplined, blue-suited El Al pilots
Who soar confidently through dappled cerulean heavens.
Od lo avda tikvatenu -
Our hope is not yet lost! *
The tongue of the prophets is heard when ordering a buttered roll,
Trying on a pair of new Nimrod sandals, arguing with a Maccabee
Games soccer referee.
Redemption of luxury, relaxation and healthful cuisine present themselves
As wiry, olive-skinned Sephardic waiters bring chopped salads with
Emek cheese for breakfast
At Jerusalem's rainbow limestone King David Hotel, favored by dignitaries–
Never again to be used as British Administrative Headquarters.
Od lo avda tikvatenu -
Our hope is not yet lost!
On Shavuot a pious writer enjoys cheesecake at a kosher café near Tel
Aviv's Dizengoff Square –
While still nimble retired policemen enjoy thwack of "matkot" paddle-
ball along the malachite Mediterranean's shoreline.
A Parisian immigrant from Le Marais remembers being pummeled for
wearing a Star of David-engraved mezuzah and knitted red kipa of re-
spectful head-covering
On his way to the Grande Synagogue de la Victoire for Sabbath worship.
Now he gets married at night under a canopy woven with blue and
white patriotic carnations
Beneath the gleaming Levantine Negev Desert sky.

Od lo avda tikvatenu -
Our hope is not yet lost!

* This refrain is a quotation from Israel's national anthem "Hatikva" — words by Naftali Herz Imber (1877).

Wounded Warriors *

Hard movement, hard speech, hard thought, hard to sleep –
Crass explosions crush, burn, batter, sever,
Altering lean, muscular Achilles
Physiques and boyish looks, leaving a
Fitful, flawed introspection to weep.
Yet grit, sweat, weights, brace, prosthesis ever
Recapture winning smile's inner graces.
Names of comrades now lost to this world? The
Mantra crams grim daydreams at toolbench, or
Punctuates tow-headed toddler's ABC's.
A May visit to Arlington's Acre
Of Sorrows for patriots brings release –
To lie here someday in a globe sans war:
Near cherry blossom balm of Lordly peace!

* Unique sonnet rhyme scheme: ABCD ABCD EFEFEF.

My Brother's Tears

My brother's tears flow for all the world's marred-pot imperfections:
When Hypatia was cut up with roof tiles in an Alexandria public square
For the "sin" of blond tresses, controlled demeanor and expert teaching
in mathematics and philosophy;
When Lisa Meitner got no Nobel recognition despite her essential calculations
Leading to Otto Hahn's nucleus-splitting Chemistry Prize in 1944;
When young, bronze-skinned lawyer Mohandas Gandhi was ejected
from a first class train compartment in Pretoria;
When refuse was hurled down on noble Jackie Robinson by baseball
bleacher fans of short-sighted bias –
My brother cried out like a victorious thoroughbred pierced with a life-
altering injury at the finish line.

My brother's tears are fused with the historic memory
of Mosaic agonies, as well:
His tears are a salve for the sweltering,
whip-lashed backs of women with child
And their men as they forage for straw to make bricks that would honor
an alien tyrant in death;
His weeping is an eternal embrace
for psalm-chanting Kohanim priests who refused
To leave the Holy Temple's inner sanctum
when Nebuchadnezzar and Vespasian
Ordered breaching of the rainbow-hued Jerusalem stone walls.
He grows lachrymose at the image of ramrod-straight officer, gentle-
man, patriot and
Polyglot Captain Alfred Dreyfus stripped of his epaulet-plumage in a
jeering parade of misdirected Gallic shame.
His waterfall of pain fills a ritual bath

that purifies the souls of day-dreaming Holocaust
Survivors haunted by the bittersweet, spectral caresses of lost first families.

My brother's tears are balm of Gilead for the virtuous pariah, taunted
sage, downtrodden
Blighted, under-appreciated Good Samaritan and virtuoso homeless in
every epoch –
But they are not shed for the lone, unpolished crystal self in isolation
from a menagerie
Of other gleaming glass unicorn citizen-figurines.

Mariner-Reverie at 91

(for Mrs. Sarah Hantman on Mother's Day, 2016)

Now is the time for sweet remembering:
Abe in white summer sailor suit on day pass,
spying Sarah at Low Library—fleeting
glimpse enough for love's quivering compass.
Bell bottoms tailed brunette to Brooklyn-bound
train. Imploring. Address exchange. Good looks,
gentle demeanor—subway diamond found?
Young Salt knew Lincoln Place neighbors: heart-hooked!

Now, too, is the season when beige throw,
gold cushions and brown sofa pillows lull –
buoying sore mortal frame and wistful soul…
USS Ault… Japan… dire surf to mull!

Widow, take comfort, a dear embrace awaits:
Your seafarer, under stone, readies; shakes.

Chagall in Crimson and White *

Cherry-red of suspended, dripping flayed ox that bellowed:
Memories of grandfather's ritual slaughtering in shtetlach.
Russian Revolution-red of banners upright and fallen,
signal disillusionment:
Artist-as-visionary did not see Lenin and violent masses as viable milieu–
So steadfast Jews who cradle maroon velvet Torahs dominate.
Carnation-red of fresh flowers picked for still life perfection
By the artist's refined, cameo-doll-face wife Bella –
She who poses in green dress with white lace cuffs and matching fan,
Who spends leisure hours translating Gallic verse into Yiddish.
Blood-red sky underneath Christ with striped Hebrew loincloth:
Reminder that victims of pogrom
and Holocaust are kin to Christendom's Savior.
Fire-red angel plummets past Sabbath candle, fleeing rabbi with Torah
scroll, gentle horse, green violin, mother cradling child, sun –
Swooping down from a heaven betrayed by man/fellow man inhuman-
ity in an uprooted sphere.
Scarlet-red of a passion goat embraced by a comely second love of with-
ering widower-hood:
Unintended consequence after daughter Ida hires a young, accom-
plished, French-speaking elder companion.
Deep claret-red of original beloved Bella's dress
in the moonlit Vitebsk night–
Newly-wed couple clasp beneath a sky lantern emanating suffused light
of innocent affection:
White veil and snowy rooftops echo purity
of soulmate palette-and-brush bonding –
Image of lifelong felicity that helped smudge chaotic imprints.
Chagall of unkind war, dizzying upheaval and illicit passion:

Weighty, vermilion-red.
But what of challenging exile's floating nostalgia?
Dabbed in details of ecstasy cream.

* "Chagall in Crimson and White" was informed by the writer's visit
to the Jewish Museum exhibit, "Chagall: Love, War, and Exile" (September 15, 2013 — February 2, 2014) and the accompanying catalogue
(Susan Tumarkin Goodman, Editor; Yale University Press).

Twilight Reverie for Jack

Smile tenderly at slender blonde woman of valor;
Clasp her hand affectionately eight times:
Once for each child, grandchild and great-grandchild
Shared over the congenial dawn-dusk calendar
Of grins, tears, reassurances, concerns and prideful whispers.

Thank the kind, efficient, muscled home nurse
Who does able lifting into and out of a wheelchair
Now that a large-boned, six-foot lionesque patriarch
Will take no more lumbering strides along Hillsboro Beach,
Or drives to the Country Club Dining Room for
Birthday and anniversary fiesta euphoria.

Lord, watch over an eminently fine family pillar:
As bodily vigor wanes, allow regal dignity to linger;
Strengthen the soul so that its merits will form
A passionate embrace to soothe faithful Archangel Gabriel
Whose presence guards Torah, Israel and blessed Eternity.

Name Tribute Sonnet: George Drummond

(for a beadle on the occasion of his stay at Bronx Lebanon Hospital)

Glowing with aura of modesty's crown;
Emissary for devotional calls.
Omniscient One's watchman — Gramercy town;
Regent soul of Little Synagogue's halls.
Goodly tribal brother sets candlesticks,
Empties closet of Torah and siddurim,
Deposits Scroll in white Ark, gets holy "kicks"
Readying wicker basket of seraphim-
Unity prayer books for proclaiming
Majesty of Almighty and Sabbath
Malka — Bride of Friday eve hymn-making.
Oh, loyal servant on the Lordly path!
Never-ending faith seals your labor's worth:
Deign to stay with us, prayer-mates on Earth!

H. Heine: Artist-Martyr

Where is the fire when once extinguished?
Where may the bygone wind be found?
(from an H. Heine love ballad)

Dreamy Düsseldorf youth in Lyceum:
Mind took flight with Jesuits' wise routines.
Millionaire uncle in Hamburg taught sums,
But romance and poesy fired this teen.
Göttingen lawyer; would-be bureaucrat –
So Hebrew morphed into Lutheran.
Reisebilder Travel Pictures by Diet
Banned; Heinrich's triumph: Parisian man!
Mathilde's saintly love, secret pension;
Lieder lyricist, eight years' mattress-grave –
"Lorelei" bard had faith of such dimension
Confessions touted worth *all* Bible sects have.
Ballad pearls' luster — irony and grief:
Artist, persevering: martyr-in-chief!

Widower Bard

(for Daniel Fernandez, Director, New York Poetry Forum)

"Dios te respecta cuando trabajas pero te ama cuando bailas"— *Proverbio Sufi*
"God respects you when you work but loves you when you dance."— *Sufi Proverb*

Carmela awaits her baile partner:
Row, row, row to reach a better Eden;
Heaven beckons a wistful widower.

Oh, proud husband, playwright, versifier!
Ivy League charmer of supreme reason –
Carmela awaits her baile partner.

Advertising colleague: Run! Swim! Flex! Stir!
True connoisseur of every season:
Heaven beckons a wistful widower.

Russo-Castilian linguist-warbler;
Gracioso as host of the maison –
Carmela awaits her baile partner.

Gotham bards' wiry jefe — rapt leader –
At Captain's Table guides mind-heart fusion:
Heaven beckons a wistful widower.

Dear friend in Golden Age: foibles to conquer –
So sprightly, feisty soul says Lord's amens.
Carmela awaits her baile partner:
Heaven beckons a wistful widower.

Savior of Blizzard Jonas

Blizzard Jonas brought feisty blasts and white-wall blankets
near January's close –
26.8 inches in Central Park, and more mountains
of heavy flakes in Big Apple's outer boroughs.
Exit taxi a long block from Bell Boulevard allergist
while enduring pedestrian woes,
For soaring curb piles of frozen-speckled ploughed slush make closer
access a future dream, as any walker knows!

Mayor De Blasio showed civility by sending snow-shoveling youth
to Bayside streets,
But clearing curbs was truly a David Blaine magician's feat:
Where to put the endless white stuff, if corner, curb, sidewalk or road
were not to be replete?
Why didn't OEM give go-ahead to ship downy urban excess to Citi
Field (which Mets in the frosty season surely do not need)?

Two widows, a divorcée and their middle-aged professional single daughters
Huddled in two-family brick-and-shingles at the end of Utopia Park-
way, near Little Neck Bay's roiling waters;
While Blizzard Jonas ranted and raved, they imbibed hot chocolate and
took in what CNN and TCM had to offer –
The next morning all scrambled for the phone number of a tall, hulking
Celt known to be a Snowstorm Savior.

That lumbering gentleman equipped with snow blower, shovels, brawn
and the patience of a saint
Is Mr. H.J. of Whitestone, bachelor with station wagon (unafraid to

give a post-Jonas lift to a North Shore nurse-neighbor whose driver's heart was faint).

With only an occasional cigarette for warmth and comfort, H.J. cleared three inundated driveways, walkways and porches without complaint – The Snowstorm Savior's hardy genes shine forth when NYC weather is quaint and unrestrained.

Marius, Deserving and Endearing *

Marius the healthy two-year-old giraffe towered
over the other gangly youngsters –
His goofy grin reflected an ever cheerful disposition.
With almost motherly solicitation,
Marius gently nudged reluctant eaters
to the food platform or mater's nipples.
His congeniality drew huddling one-year-olds
Who invariably rubbed against their comforting, tawny, striped Gul-
liver of Gibralter.

Marius hailed from the Copenhagen Zoo –
A giraffe-breeding institution that took its stewardship role very seriously.
A genetic sample was taken from the happy-go-lucky giraffe
Whom some of the efficient, highly disciplined zookeepers found to
be a bit overbearing.
Ja vol, kommandant!
Marius had "common genes": unexceptional, ordinary;
Breeding him with available females would produce redundant, possibly
sickly offspring.
Never mind that a kind-hearted billionaire had offered to pay fifty
thousand euros ransom
To rescue Marius from his eugenics mill stall,
Or that the Yorkshire Wildlife Park yearned to have him as denizen –
Whether as doting father or charming bachelor uncle.
Marius was simply a useless eater –
A surplus luftmensche and firing squad candidate
Daring to take up Lebensraum that belonged to his betters.
Without doubt, a solution needed to be executed post-haste:
Apply excruciating bolt gun to Marius's trusting brain –

Thus keeping his tender flesh pure and poison-free –
Then butcher, chop, feed good bloody protein to lions,
Ensuring shiny hair and strong teeth for the ultimate predator.
All this as fair Scandinavian children took in the girafficide with incredulous fascination:
An animal refuge had suddenly become a lager for a ferocious survival-of-the-fittest public display.

Marius, I have photos of your wacky face and endearing form
Bordered with stickers depicting the blond, red-headed and raven-haired children who will never know you
On the mirror of my guest bedroom,
With its table of houseplants, Bootsie snapshot, iMac and white and gold Marie Antoinette French Provincial furniture.
How deserving you are of the daily bittersweet Anne Frank smile
I cast your way.

* This tribute to Marius the ill-fated Danish giraffe was informed by February, 2014 online articles and photographs by journalists and photographers from The Guardian, CBC/Reuters, Mail Online and The Economist.

IV. WIVES & LASSES

Grandma Lena

(Inspired by Nellie Wong's pantoum, "Grandmother's Song")

Rice kugel simmering in pan
Soft touch on brow of girl or boy
Pullet boiled in broth — no can –
Singer for seamstress's employ.

Soft touch on brow of girl or boy
Patient as Mother Teresa
Singer for seamstress's employ
Sabbath kindling balabusta.

Patient as Mother Teresa
With hale or ill, adult or child
Sabbath kindling balabusta
A Yiddish voice, gentle and mild.

With hale or ill, adult or child
The lokshen cure—fine way to dine
A Yiddish voice, gentle and mild
Sang shtetl lullabies divine.

The lokshen cure — fine way to dine
The cook, dear ancestress, fled Czar
Sang shtetl lullabies divine
Sans "spasiba" and samovar.

The cook, dear ancestress, fled Czar
Hadassah cribs her charity

Sans "spasiba" and samovar
The Holy Land — spry devotee.

Hadassah cribs her charity
Almond eyes spied pushka's power
The Holy Land — spry devotee
Smile, Zion's newborns' comforter!

Almond eyes spied pushka's power
High-cheekboned Grandma dusts divan
Smile, Zion's newborns' comforter!
Rice kugel simmering in pan…

Ethics of the Mothers

Don't allow your husband to be privy to angst shared with trusty therapist–
Else your marriage license may be a mere memory sorely to be missed!

Girlfriends with ulterior motives undermine the industrious woman of valor–
Shake them loose like barnacles eroding a secure dock's wooden matter.

A bookish mother with a baseball hitter should learn to use a mitt;
An aspiring soccer mom with a little Martha Stewart ought to master
soufflés, and knit.

Inner beauty shows itself in pleasant conversation, compassion, pa-
tience, generosity and reluctance to blame;
It is what will make a spouse sing out in the shower,
"Ba Mir Bistu Shein!" *

Cultivate an attractive appearance with haircut, manicure, pedicure,
make-up, jewelry and a stylish, flattering frock –
But know that these don't replace sterling character as wrinkles appear
(marked by passing years and clock).

Fidelity is faithfulness to one partner—near or far — in a committed
relationship or marriage;
Practice it for decades and you've triumphed; one slip, a sacrilege!
A house filled with the voices of helpmate and children who enjoy
healthful home-cooking at a table consecrated by the Lord
Is God's gifted rose bestowed as a woman's greatest reward!

* "Ba Mir Bistu Shein" is a popular song with both Yiddish and English
lyrics; the title means "To Me You Are Beautiful." Its Big Band era

recordings ranged from The Andrews Sisters to Ella Fitzgerald. Composer Sholom Secunda was paid only $30 for the future swing hit, a fee that he had to split with the lyricist.

Profile and Silhouette

(Inspired by "The Mexican Hat Dance")

Profile, profile, profile:
The delicate cameo.
Profile, profile, profile:
Flamenco dancer's ruffled dress.
The silhouette of a comely maiden,
The silhouette of a gentle peasant:
Each one is pleasing to God –
Each one in a unique way.

Profile, profile, profile:
Hair arranged in a great bun.
Profile, profile, profile:
The geisha bows before us.
The silhouette of her kimono,
The silhouette of the brave Samurai:
Each one is pleasing to God –
Each one in a unique way.

Profile, profile, profile:
Jazz lady approaches the piano.
Profile, profile, profile:
Her afro moves with the notes.
The silhouette of an Indian flautist,
The silhouette of jugglers:
Each one is pleasing to God –
Each one in a unique way.

Profile, profile, profile:
The beard of a wise old man.
Profile, profile, profile:
The soprano and her shawl.
The silhouette of graceful Moorish arches,
The silhouette of lofty Gothic arches:
Each one is pleasing to God –
Each one in a unique way.

El perfil y la silueta

(Inspirado por El jarabe tapatío)

Perfil, perfil, perfil:
El camafeo fino.
Perfil, perfil, perfil:
El traje de flamenca.
La silueta de la moza bella,
La silueta del rústico manso:
A Dios le gusta cada uno –
Cada uno con su propio estilo.

Perfil, perfil, perfil:
El pelo en gran moño.
Perfil, perfil, perfil:
La geisha se inclina.
La silueta de su kimono,
La silueta del samurai bravo:
A Dios le gusta cada uno –
Cada uno con su propio estilo.

Perfil, perfil, perfil:
La jazz acerca al piano.
Perfil, perfil, perfil:
Su afro se mueve con los tonos.
La silueta del flautist indio,
La silueta de los malabaristas:
A Dios le gusta cada uno –
Cada uno con su propio estilo.

Perfil, perfil, perfil:
La Barba del sabio.
Perfil, perfil, perfil:
La soprano y su mantón.
La silueta de los arcos moros de gracia,
La silueta de los arcos góticos de altura:
A Dios le gusta cada uno –
Cada uno con su propio estilo.

Ode to a Teak Desk

(Inspired by Joy Harjo's poem, "Perhaps the World Ends Here")

Married life begins at a teak desk –
Chosen at an Upper East Side Danish furniture store
With cultivated Hungarian-Jewish refugee spouse.
At the teak desk syllabi were typed for
Freshman Composition classes at Jersey City's Hudson County College
Taught by newly-wed adjunct commuting from
Modest Parkchester Bronx apartment-den of cozy bliss.

The life of a young, childless divorcee begins at a teak desk –
"Types of Transitions" and "A Smorgasbord of Punctuation" were cre-
ated for Fundamentals of Writing classes at South Bronx's Gompers
High School
Taught by a wistful, pining heart bicycling to work from
Bronx Park East flat across from Botanical Garden and Zoo.

The life of a sedate retiree and middle-aged writer begins at a teak desk–
The green report cover holds verse for the New York Poetry Forum
Central Park Picnic;
The orange report cover secures poems for the Kew Gardens Com-
munity Center Bella Goldworth Tribute;
The purple report cover clasps Rosh Hashanah outpourings for the Lit-
tle Synagogue Kabbalat Shabbat service;
The red oak tag folder cradles Fresh Meadows Poets' Corresponding
Secretary's disseminations of bardic activities, and verse offerings.
The clear plastic zip case embraces Harry Ellison's Poet's Circle lecture
notes with their folk-universal brotherhood charm.

The life of eternal reward for forbearance will surely begin
At a teak desk cluttered with dear memorabilia:
Yellow Moulin Roty kaleidoscope, maroon enamel bird motif letter
opener, waterway stones used as paperweights,
Small, gold-framed photo of the author clasping her black-and-white
Chihuahua mutt,
Seated on living room sofa next to handsome, cancer-ridden Semitic father.
The silver-and-gray Cross pen clattered when the ultimate poem of an
oeuvre was finished –
Thus concluding perceptions of outright beauty — and irritations –
That induced Tahitian pearls of never-out-of-thought eloquence
Jotted down in floral journals pressed against a red blotter
Leaning on the spacious top of a beloved honey blond,
Scandinavian teak desk –
Posterity's charitable gift to a lone scrivener lass:
The Lord's ward – now ambling in a teak forest paradise.

The Meaning of It All...

I wish that my tombstone would say:
"The burden of the elect"
The burden of shame teaches the lesson
Of humility as holy as pain endured
By martyrs of the faith.

I wish my friends' tombstones to say:
"Dear widower, widow, bachelor, spinster and companion-poets
Of she the unfortunate one (yet sweet, generous and angelic) –
You merit the halcyon sky sans clouds of anxious inconstancy –
Because your loyalty won against pernicious social prejudice:
The stain and stigma that embraced the shivering body
Of the elect friend."

Buying enchanting gifts to send to children of the family every month;
Writing sublime verse in order to paint life with dabs of gentleness;
Visiting glorious museums to appreciate possible heights
of the human soul and mind:
These softened my implacable burden as the weary chosen one –
That is I:
She with fracture and nobility in an all-too-tender heart.

La significancia de lo todo...

Quiero que mi lápida sepulcral dijese:
"La carga de la elegida."
La carga de la vergüenza muestra la lección
De humildad tan sagrada coma el dolor soportado
Por los mártires de la fé.

Quiero que la lápida sepulcral de mis amigos dijese:
"Queridos viúdos, solteros y compañeros-poetas
De ella la desafortunada (ya dulce, generosa y angélica) –
Ustedes merecen el cielo apacible sin las nubes ansiosas e inconstantes–
Porque su lealtad venció contra el pernicioso perjuicio social:
La mancha y el estigma que abrazaron al tembloroso cuerpo
De la amiga elegida."

Comprando los regalos encantadores para mandar a los niños de la familia cada mes;
Escribiendo los versos exaltados para pintar la vida con pequeñas cantidades de bondad;
Visitando los museos gloriosos para apreciar las alturas posibles del alma y la mente humana:
Estos hicieron más suave mi carga implacable como la elegida fatigada–
Esa soy yo:
Ella con las fracturas y la nobleza en un corazón demasiado tierno.

Acceptance

Accord that embraces the wretched woman
When winners of life's lottery
Don't practice the slights and contempt that are encouraged
In a culture of judgments superfluous and harsh –
Of censures as sharp as the teeth of a hungry snake –
This lack of implementation of presumed superiority –
A presumption not sanctioned by God –
This brave, kind, just sensibility
Is true, blessed acceptance:
That which is well known by both angels and mortal souls
Who have risen to a heavenly plain without barbs.

La aceptación

El acuerdo que acaricia a la desgraciada
Cuando los ganadores de la lotería de la vida
No practican los desaires y el desprecio que se alientan
En una cultura de los juicios superfluos y ásperos –
De las censuras tan agudas corno los dientes de una culebra hambrienta –
Esta falta de implementación de la superioridad presumida –
Una presunción no sancionada por Dios –
Esta sensibilidad brava, bondadosa y justa
Es la aceptación verdadera y bendita:
Lo que saben bien ambos los ángeles y las almas mortales
Que han subido a una pradera celeste sin las púas.

Mother Chides

"Your poet friends inhabit foolish bubbles;
Harry is smothered by your kindness.
Flash Nature's Jewelry for cash troubles;
Long rebbetzin skirts don't define piousness. *

Hebrew Gift World, Dress Barn, Rite Aid—no more
Without *your* buying. Barnes & Noble, too,
In the black due to mishugga addict-lure. **
That second piece of bread you'll live to rue!

Brown ducks charm when you row with fragile Dan;
Don't capsize in toxic red algae bloom!
Foreign ciné with Nita, avid fan –
Eight-dollar escapes plus cabs will seal your doom!"

Mother: chide, excoriate me ever –
Survive without your sachel? Never! ***

* "Rebbetzin" — Yiddish for "rabbi's wife".
** "Mishugga" — Yiddish for "senseless".
* * * "Sachel" — Yiddish for "common sense".

Glossary for "Senior Memory Cascade" Sonnet Sequence

1. Commager — Henry Steele Commager, distinguished historian and professor of American history whose texts were widely used by college students in the 1940's
2. macher — someone proud of being an achiever, or a "mover and a shaker" with social status (Yiddish)
3. shul — informal, affectionate word for synagogue (Yiddish)
4. Tilden — Tilden High School (a public New York City high school for students living in the area where Crown Heights and Bedford-Stuyvesant intersect in Brooklyn)
5. mishpacha — family (Yiddish and Hebrew)
6. kvell — to swell with pride and joy, as over a child's accomplishments (Yiddish)
7. halacha — Jewish law (e.g. regarding keeping the Sabbath, eating kosher food, etc.)
8. Mello Roll — a rolled up ice cream candy treat available in movie theaters from the 1930's – 1950's
9. geshmakteh — delicious (it can be used in the context of food or a delightful experience); Yiddish
10. tate — father (Yiddish)
11. maidelas — young, unmarried females (Yiddish)

Senior Memory Cascade I

(for Mrs. Sarah Hantman, family matriarch)

My nonagenarian mom-protector
emerges from shower a "clean goil";
Then cascade memories of Kurinsky toil:
Commager texts shared with rabbi's daughter;
White satin gown that Ethel also wore.
Big macher Relief man made Papa boil:
"Two daughters. Two jobs, now!" Oy, a thought to roil!
Sleep on pull-out sofa: living room no more.

Bubbie Batsheva in Corner Shul: pledges
dollar from the "woman of good name"; in
hospital, after Tilden, you spooned
her soup. "Sabbath levity is a sin!"
She slipped you her gold band, and chided –
You lost her widow's seal raking near hedges.

Senior Memory Cascade II

Kurinsky daughters of Lincoln Place rose
from Brooklyn College to Ivy laurels:
Columbia, Yale welcomed wartime gals.
Papa went off Relief— almost froze his toes;
Two hours by train to Fort Monmouth — tax guides
for Signal Corps his math whiz specialty. New
colleagues were Irishmen: hamish, tall, blue-
eyed folk. Hot meals after schmoozy rides:
Lena made tzimmes, kugels, chicken soup.
Abe, on leave from Battleship Ault, found love:
Sarah perusing books in Low Library.
Rachel's bashert tinkled the ivories,
cradled tomes, trilled Spanish: So above!
Depression times linked geshmakteh loops.

Senior Memory Cascade III

Mama schlepped to East New York: flour
bags on dole. She gifted some to Tanta
Ida, Esther, Shirley, Dave — mishpacha
from Mogilev Gobernya… shtetl dour –
could smile and kvell with FDR in power.
Uncle Simon: white-shirted printer, a
stern man crowned with Torah halacha,
gave out quarters for gelt at golden hour
when lit menorah blazed in his kitchen
window. Kinder dreamed of Mello-Rolls,
Garbo, Kay Francis, Barrymores, Gable
and remembered Valentino's pull.
Mama's grandson and Dave's son: physicians!
Through schooling, New World crafts uplifted souls.

Senior Memory Cascade IV

Papa's tate Shmuel had TB, so
kindness from London nurses was his New
World haven. Bubbie Batsheva didn't rue
scrimping kopeks, choosing the kinder, woe
of steerage, ocean separation, blow
that newsstand hawking left Papa ice-blue –
no calculus for a teen with mind so true.
As self-taught accountant Papa showed,
by test, he knew as much as college grads.
Clear plastic runners on green rose carpet
kept the apartment clean at tax season.
Papa's hunger for words was the reason
a Gulliver-sized Webster's was set
on closet shelf. A decimal wit it adds.

Senior Memory Cascade V

Papa was Kiev-born — never wished
Czar "spaciba" as few bright Jewish boys
glimpsed university gates (banned
by numerus clausus). In New York, joys
included devouring many papers:
Times, Tribune, Sun, Mirror, Daily Worker…
In his native land, Socialist capers
were intriguing — but New Deal inputs would stir
heart of a loyal Democrat. Still, J.
Edgar took umbrage at breadth of reading –
Papa had to swear love for U.S.A.,
WPA job at Fort Monmouth preserving.
New World liberties had their limits for
A Russky-Jew employed in time of war.

Senior Memory Cascade VI

Mama, a Tucker: seamstress from shtetl
near Orsha Junction. White Russian nobleman-
physician: a pogrom-preventing lamb.
Mama left with sister Ida to settle,
meeting kindly Morris at a lecture.
Her maidelas she brought thermos, sandwiches
at shoemaker near Crown Heights school. Bless her!
Mama pleaded with Anglo schoolmarm misses:
"*Don't yell at mein tochters! They are gutte
kinderlach.*" Harried educators sighed:
"We raise our voices to the restless herd –
Disparagement was not at all implied!"
Hindela — too young to leave *her* mutter –
perished in Einsatzgruppen's lethal stir.

Senior Memory Cascade VII

Abe's parents: kissing cousin proprietors
Of Main Cloak Company, Main Street, Freehold town –
Wooden cart wound through store, round and round:
Brothers Izzy and Lou gave rides to kinder.
Main Cloak coats, solely, Police Chief's pert wife wore –
Gifts at Christmastime so lads would not hound
Dreamy Abe, high school editor, homeward-bound –
Headed for gray porch hammock-swing's allure…
Old white frame nestled on Manalapan,
Also home to sister Dottie who drew
Curious stares for raven hair and eyes
Brown as burnt onions that did not match the skies.
On USS Ault, buddy Bill Hackmann knew
That sufferings of youth could plague a man.

Senior Memory Cascade VIII

Monmouth State Teacher's College: Abe's widower
English professor sobbed at Dover
Beach's "darkling plain"; Abe "Romeo-ed" her
so many co-eds that no dates for rover
could be found. High school English teacher, then
elementary school, guidance, A.P. –
Daughter opened Board of Ed letter when
it was too late: principal, posthumously.
Abe's Main Cloak Company inheritance
squandered via brother-in-law's trips
to Caribbean paradises. Hence,
"Zero from zero is zero" quip.
Unjust straw mementos haunt the Whitestone house –
Still, Abe's smiles, wise jokes, prayers, goodness rouse.

Senior Memory Cascade IX

Sarah taught tough teen gals at Erasmus
High — "Write soldier beaus—tell them world news now!"
At Corona's PS 92 just
Irish principals: Maguire, Murphy wowed
by near insubordinations ethics
caused—as when she wouldn't admonish
"Sloppy handwriting!" for ironic trick
on CP girl's report card. Enough heart-squish!
Now school librarian, Sarah found tales
with light of inner beauty, self-worth's blaze:
Plain Russian peasant mother's looks will regale.
Langston's verse, Stevie's loving coos: gifted race!
"My Yiddishe Momme" assemblies drew tears –
Teacher, too, knew poverty, bias, fear.

Senior Memory Cascade X

Molly and Izzy gave Sarah three-gold-
bird pendant: Stuart, Barry, Barbara.
Stu: to grandchildren, zany, attentive "Pa";
radiologist in awe of Bible's hold.
Barry: good-hearted, resourceful, upright mold
cradles bioengineer son and his ma,
balm for homebound students: downcast to "Rah!"
Special Ed screenplays to Weinstein — foibles told
as Hantman scribbler-tenderness allows.
Barbara taught language arts in ghettos,
versified the call of Abraham's kin;
friendship trumped romance (help surviving woes) –
humility saved the least one's skin.
To heal the world, cultivate such darling boughs!

Ninetieth

(for Mrs. Sarah Hantman, family matriarch, on becoming a "nonagenarian")

Never-ending nurturing of a lioness nudging three cubs and charming progeny
Indomitable force with intension to protect, shelter and inspire
None can compete as teacher, school librarian and builder of a feath-
ered nest at home
Excellence reached via conscientious effort with egalitarian chance for all
Thorough, down-to-earth thoughtfulness that never forgets a detail
Integrity of honesty infused with tact for enlightenment never intended
to be impolite
Eager to elevate through insights based on facts,
inferences and common sense
Trainer with talking, example and wisdom of a gray-haired thinker
Hallelujah for hour of Hantman matriarch's ninety haimeshe spring-
times on HaShem's awesome sphere!

Sonnet for Sarah

(Dedicated to Mrs. Sarah Hantman two years after her personal philosophy revealing, "fanudjit" surgery at North Shore Hospital, Manhasset) *

Salty-words senior knows true character
in a flash. If ominous, lioness
Nonagenarian matriarch stirs –
Sheltering her pride from heart-sting duress.

Advice overflows her wise riverbanks:
"God does *not* want us to be schlemiels!"
"Secret protectors schlep in righteous flanks."
"Choose down-to-earth: never luftmensch unreal!" **

Tentative-gait believer is hush-hush
about gratitude to God. Cautious, she
Clings to small circle — not yentas who push;
Treasures honest opponent above phony.

Gray hair and cane with childless daughter face
Sweet fate after joys: soul from place to Place.

* fanudgit — Yiddish for "bothersome" and "uncomfortable"
** luftmensch — Yiddish for a person who expects to live off the "air";
that is, an impractical being whose ability to survive is in question due
to insufficient grounding in down-to-earth exigencies

Sleeping Treasures

Gold-dipped opera glasses, gift of my tender-hearted dad;
A huge straw hat with flirtatious red ribbon band;
Diamond-and-gold cocktail ring in the shape of a carnation that my
Aunt Rachel left me;
Gaudy green-and-red Scotch plaid cape that came from my grandpar-
ent's New Jersey store;
A strapless black velvet New Year's dress and matching bolero jacket.

I have these lovely, sentimental things resting in drawer and trunk,
Or hanging in closets while shouting abandonment –
An exile that much more poignant because of their coddled prior status.

Before was the capricious life of their owner –
The youth of an English teacher in depressed neighborhoods of a rainbow city;
Before were memories of teaching *Romeo and Juliet* to child-students
of fourteen,
And going out with a dignified, appealing faculty member dressed in a
three-piece suit.

Now is a life as simple as that of a saitly nun in her beloved convent –
An existence full of soulful passion – with the whole rose-colored world
As its splendid aim.

Los tesoros durmientes

Las gafas para la ópera bañadas en oro, regalo de mi tierno papá;
Un sombrero de paja grandísimo con una cinta roja y coqueta;
El anillo cóctel de oro y diamantes del tamaño de un clavel que me dejó
mi tía Raquel;
La capa de manta escocesa en verde y rojo chillón que vino de la tienda
de mis abuelos en New Jersey;
Un vestido negro para el Año Nuevo de terciopelo, sin tiras, y una cha-
queta bolero haciendo juego.

Yo tengo estas cosas preciosas y sentimentales descansando en cajónes
y baúles,
O colgando en los roperos mientras daban gritos de abandono –
Un destierro aún más conmovedor a causa de su acariciado pasado.

Antes era la vida caprichosa de su dueña—
La juventud de una maestra de lengua inglesa
En los barrios deprimidos de una ciudad luminosa;
Antes eran los recuerdos de enseñar Romeo y Julieta a los adorables
inocentes estudiantes de catorce años,
Y salir con un compañero de la facultad digno y atractivo en su traje
con chaleco.

Ahora es una vida tan sencilla como la de una monja santa en su convento querido –
Una existencia de pasión llena de sentimientos – con todo el mundo color de rosa
Como su espléndido objetivo.

Sixty-One

Eyes have already imbibed three-quarters of all
Lanky daffodils of springtime blossoming.
Ears have heard sounds as diverse as raucous seagulls honking
for fish entrails
Behind a filleter's Manhattan Beach trawler
And speckled ducks cooing gently for handfuls of corn while perched
on boulders
Along Pittsford's Erie Canal promenade.
Ken has experienced honeyed, "*I love you very, very, very much*" of dear
Sacred ablution-healthy repast-Torah study companion –
And see-saw vertigo of scheister manipulation.

Upright mahogany Sohmer piano has been bequeathed to
Great-nephew who will continue to press its keys with respectful intensity
To the steady metronome beat of largo, andante or allegro
After great-aunt has been liberated from harmonies and dissonances
Of this Vale of Tears.

At sixty-one, begin the letting go of things and disappointments –
Sound the ram's horn for renewal by a neophyte salvation-generation
Needed to spread the balm of primordial balance
On our noble, blue marble Earth.

Lorelei of Little Neck Bay

(After Heinrich Heine's poem, "Loreleylied")

Denizens of Whitestone and Bayside
Feel an eerie, haunting pang
For an ancient age when did abide
Bark-hut dwellers who splashed and sang.
The crisp fall breeze stirs blue topaz waves,
And choppily flows the bay –
Burnished sunset at King's Point craves
Another sunrise-above-willows day.

Bay Maiden of raven tress floats high
Above Little Neck Bay's sapphire bowl;
Her turkey feather headband sailors spy –
Red-beaded moccasins bind their souls.

In deer dress, she paddles well above shores –
A taut canoe her cloudless throne.
She chants an Algonquin tune—then roar
Old Salts in frigates, who later moan.

Nearly doomed in their floundering sloops,
Mariners stop their ears with wax;
Bayside Marina then beckons the duped –
Once anchored, all hands relax.

Bay Maiden is a gentle echo
Of a time when virgin inlets pulsed;
May the living ocean bow, and bestow
Her white headdress of purity and trust.

Others Just Couldn't See...

The black waiter in Mississippi smiled broadly at the rude, pallid politician
Though his dark eyes revealed a tremendous sadness:
Others just couldn't see...
At the elegant, restricted hotel a rich Jewish woman who paid extra to
avoid her fate
Lived to hear the swimming pool refilled after her jubilant swim:
Others just couldn't see...
The enchanting daughter of a tavern owner in a university town
Fell in love with a student prince who liked to drink her father's beer
and toast the world –
But his relatives insisted on a frigid, elitist wedding:
Others just couldn't see...
A young Dane philosophized, fenced and feigned madness as protection against
The corrupt court of his uncle — assassin and usurper:
Others just couldn't see...
The almost-always-an-understudy actress with qualities to stand out
and dazzle a jaded public –
Others just couldn't see!

Los otros apenas pudieron ver...

El camarero de raza negra en Mississippi sonrió ampliamente al rudo y
pálido político
Aunque sus ojos oscuros mostraron una tremenda tristeza:
Los otros apenas pudieron ver...
En el elegante y restringido hotel una mujer rica y judía que pagó más
para evitar su destino
Vivió oír la piscina rellenada después de su natación jubilosa:
Los otros apenas pudieron ver...
La hija encantadora del dueño de una taberna en un pueblo universitario
Se enamoró de un príncipe estudiante al que le gustaba beber la cerveza
de su padre y brindar por el mundo –
Pero sus parientes insistieron en una boda frígida y élitista:
Los otros apenas pudieron ver...
Un danés joven filosofó, espadeó y fingió locura como protección contra
La corte corrupta de su tío — un asesino y usurpador:
Los otros apenas pudieron ver...
La actriz casi siempre suplente con calidad para destacar y deslumbrar
a un público rendido –
¡Los otros apenas pudieron ver!

Las Desdichadas and the Seasons *

In winter las desdichadas pine with the polar bear –
They are no stranger to a shrinking habitat that requires frigid, exhaust-
ing, gulping swims with no tundra in sight.

In springtime las desdichadas hold vigils
for sparrows tumbled from their cozy nests –
What is broken, dashed or crushed spurs
on many a melancholy siren ululation.

In summer las desdichadas remember graceful graveyard ships
on the parched Aral Sea –
Thirsty enchanting ghosts populate their cosmos of withered hopes, too.

In autumn las desdichadas are pained when bulbous orange gourds
grown moldy fuel bonfires –
For stale dreams can be consumed in a conflagration of infernal misgivings.

In every season las desdichadas sleep fitfully –
Like a favorite wife with a never-opened womb,
Or a daughter condemned to exile by a warrior-father prone to rash oaths.

In every mild, sandy season, las desdichadas shelter under and embrace
the sweetly-perfumed eucalyptus –
Its aroma evokes memories safely locked
in youth's jade jewel box of possibilities:
A treasure trove las desdichadas will never allow
to be stolen or compromised –
No matter how tattered their flowered, paisley, striped, checkered
or solid shawls become.

* Las desdichadas — Spanish for the "unfortunate women."

V. JEWELS OF CREATION

Seasonal Flashback Nonets *

Springtimes in Whitestone

Purple-blue hydrangea blooms nod;
Squat hostas spill over walkway;
White petunias: planted
In gray patio urn –
Greet dawn along with
Arborvitae,
Red maple.
Garden –
June!

Summer of '76

Sizzle — Acapulco's pristine beach;
Indigenous sellers show goods:
Tooled leather sun god bags,
Striped woven rugs, throws.
Ponchos back and forth
Barbed wire tops
Hotel pool.
Frenzy:
Poor!

Autumn of '69

"Stop the War!" flyers, black armbands, leaves
Swirling at Bayside train station
LIRR passengers
Smile, scowl at teens' jitters:
Siblings facing Draft.
Acorns come fall
Reassure
Can't you,
Too?

Winter of '61

Visit Amish Country (bitter cold):
Guide in cape and woolen bonnet.
One-room schoolhouse looks cozy;
Boiling maple syrup,
Butter brickle cones,
Pot belly stove.
Horse buggy,
Snow fields.
Neat!

* Nonet — A nine-line poetic form with the first line being assigned nine syllables, the second line eight syllables, and so forth, so that the ninth line is one syllable long. Rhyme is optional.

Little Neck Bay: Now, and Then

(Inspired by Jane Kenyon's poem, "Let Evening Come")

Let adventurers in sailboats and motorboats navigate sapphire ripples
After they launch from moorings near Bayside Marina's boardwalk.

Let seagulls flap in white-ark formations,
Smugly soar above a foraging Great Blue Heron
Whose dagger-bill, swan-neck and gossamer stalk-legs
Grace bay sand fringed by gray boulders and marshland.

Let Lover's Lane with its canopy of weeping willows give way to
earthen bicycle path,
Then Fort Totten jetty for daring hopscotch-on-stones childhood scrambles:
A jetty that hosts Irish anglers and Asian fisher folk with their pails of fluke–
Gems caught in the shadows of the Throg's Neck Bridge.

Let a beer-drinking kayaker off King's Point reel in a hefty striped bass–
Proudly displaying "this baby" to fellow paddlers hailing from:
Great Neck, Little Neck, Douglaston, Bayside and Whitestone –
Scenic towns that adorn the bay's perimeter
Like trophy wives dressed to the nines.

Let dining couples toast with Asti within white stucco, beneath green gables
Nestled near intersection of Clearview Golf Course, bridge and bay.
They enjoy Chef Pintabona's "Pasta Al Forno Zio Vincenzo"
As ghosts of former tenants Rudolph Valentino and Mayor La Guardia
Silently emote and garrulously smile with Jazz Age vigor.

Let it be known!
The bay has suffered a deeper loss of civilization in its time –
For Matinecock Algonquins cannot be seen traversing its pure waters
in birchbark canoes,
Gathering delectable quahog clams,
Nursing those of tender years in squat forest wigwams beyond the bog:
Beaming, bare-breasted squaws and protective, agile, feathered hunter-fathers
No longer bathe, wash, splash with their offspring — unafraid –
On its pristine, all-purpose beach.

May this blue topaz chipped by European conquest
and effluvium of industrial hubris
Still sparkle in its lesser glory.

Autumn Harvest: Season of Kindly Departures

Crisp apples, bulbous pumpkins: red, orange:
Autumn bounty charms folks in orchard or
Viny patch. Oaken gifts of acorn range
From earthen paths to purple-heathered moors.
Chrysanthemums make maroon, gold displays
To grace verandas' terra cotta planters.
Late September is for vineyard forays –
Tart indigo Concords will fill decanters.
Gnat-starved swallows roost in bent willows
Before adieus to nippy winds of fall;
Nightingales won't stay to assuage our woes,
But modest thrushes take pity on this lull.
Harvest's a time of ripe departures tied
With kindly stalks — Creation's wistful guides!
Viny patch. Oaken gifts of acorn range
On earthen paths. Oh, purple-heathered moors!

The Copper Beech

(for Tu B'Shevat 5775, and in deference to the passing of long-term
Little Synagogue member Gerson Goodman)

With auburn leaves that beguiled like garnets shifting with gusting wind,
Or teased like chestnut-colored dybbuks playing in dappled sun and shadow;
With branches as sturdy and numerous as Jacob's sons,
A brown-gray trunk as broad as the equator,
Roots that stretched and stretched in veins and tangles like Samson's
righteous, straining arms –
The copper beech near Little Neck Bay watched over gentle Algonquin
Indians who snuggled in bark huts,
Pleased Revolutionary War patriot Francis Lewis as he trotted by,
mounted on his favorite roan,
Looked on quizzically as paved roads replaced earthen paths and blue-
gray cobblestones,
Winked at sprouting trolley and railroad tracks,
Pumped oxygen to cleanse the air as dapper Irishmen's Model T's clat-
tered down the acorn-lined street.
The copper beech smiled when a new brick-and-shingle home was built
for a Brooklyn-Jewish WWII Navy G.I. and his family,
Destined to live for decades under its jasper crown.
The tree's leaves greeted them with congenial jostling –
Though its vast root system felt pinched
by the new home's cement foundation.
Eastern European grandparent ballplaying memories, graduation pic-
tures, book publication photos:
All took place in the glorious vicinity
of the dignified front lawn copper beech.

One summer the noble tree's carmine leaves shrivelled
like smoldering banshees,
Cascading to leave a canopy as naked as veilless Vashti dancing for King
Achashverosh and his leering courtiers.
Mother and daughter tearfully raked ruined ruby remnants,
Vowing to plant a graceful Norwegian red maple in its place to echo
copper majesty.
Those charmed by the venerable beech always see it when they look at
the fledgling maple –
For longevity, soulful sweep, breadth of feeling, Lordly understanding
Are the copper beech's compelling, eternally superior,
maroon life-force claims
On the head-bowed sons and daughters of man.

Bayside Winter Scene

Red earmuffs, scarf, coat add cheer to background
Of choppy green waves and snow-encrusted
Wooden railings above boulders that bound
Little Neck Bay, with curving blue bridge just
A quarter mile in the icicle-dangle
Distance. Vivaldi's of Valentino
Fame flaunts holly wreaths, ivory gables –
With purple winter cabbages below.
White swans that circled bulrush swamp are gone;
Chestnut wood ducks eager for bread in fall:
No show! Mournful seagulls fly from tepid sun –
This avian dearth could spread a frozen pall.
What's left to ogle casts God's poignant sheen:
Appreciate the charm of frosty scenes!

Gifts of Early April

In early April my mother will experience her 91st birthday.
She refuses to receive another charming beige, blue or green gilt-edged
tree-of-life brooch;
She scoffs at the prosaic prospect of a Macy's or Lord & Taylor gift certificate–
Though by permitting such indulgence she could augment an impressive collection of floral silk scarves.
Now the truest boons are found in the open air, close to home, leaning
on her near-senior-citizen daughter's empathetic arm:
Yolk-yellow and lemon-yellow daffodils planted by tender little hands
are spied while shuffling down Utopia Parkway near P.S. 209;
The festive yellow forsythia bell blooms
of bushes that festoon Clearview Gardens
Echo nature's palette and shout out early springtime euphoria
to the gray-haired pair.

A birthday in the season of purple crocus, verdant Passover parsley and
hard-boiled or pastel-tinted eggs
Of renewed hope eternally bequeathed to soil and mankind
Is nature's sublime, infallible annual present
For a nonagenarian born in "the cruelest month" –
With percolating, rainbow-hued signs of kindnesses yet to come.

Whitestone Springtime Haiku

Carvel's forsythia:
Row of lemon-yellow bells –
Ice cream for the eyes.

P.S. 209:
Daffodils in yolk-yellow –
Wordsworth's charmers live.

Rosa's garden blooms:
Pink-red tulips, pale crocus –
Sleepy heads waken.

Mid-Utopia:
White dogwood divider trees –
Parkway of angels.

Bay-bird dunkers splash:
White seagulls, swans; brown geese, ducks –
Sapphire water baths.

Bay rocks bulge like whales:
Elephant-gray boulders cling –
Suckle jade-green edge.

Bay fishermen stand,
Flicking lines from stone jetty –
Striped bass flounders… Oh, no!

Than-Bauks for Springtime Flora *

Harbinger Sweethearts
Daffodil blooms
Crocus swoons — March
Makes room for pairs.

Forsythia: Short-Lived Eye-Feast
Yellow bell sprays
Soft displays please
Hoo-rays! (month's joy).

Tulip Relationships
Tulips touch heads
Yellow weds pink
Deep red's the queen.

Rose of Sharon: Holy Land Prize
White, orchid-like
Jezreel hike's gem –
Pluck tyke's treasure.

Anemone: Gentle Wildflower
Red clover, wild
Bouquet child picks
Hill's mild rouge-crop.

Hydrangea: On the Move
Wind-jostled fronds;
Purple wands sway.
Blue bonds nudge, swish.

* A Than-Bauk is a three-line poem of Burmese origin with four-sylla-ble lines and rhyme on the fourth syllable of the first line, third syllable of the second line and second syllable of the third line. This is known as "rising rhyme."

The Bejewelled World

Life happens in a sapphire place:
See hyacinth petals of debutante springtime;
Look at the rainbow sky after mature summer rain;
Enjoy Mediterranean blue from Bardot's Riviera
To the zany parades of Tel Aviv –
With their divine, turqoise ecstasy.

Life happens in an emerald place:
See lush grass of a Catskills bungalow colony;
Look at imposing evergreens
that were Hansel and Gretel's trustworthy parents;
Enjoy weeping willow leaves that bow down and caress a mint-colored lake.

Life happens in a tiger's eye place:
See brown and beige fields of the Holy Land;
Look at ancient, dark peat where leprechauns played in suits of gold;
Enjoy ebony Arabian stallions galloping over sands
Of a desert that would have been forlorn without their defiant hooves.

The bejewelled world in which we find ourselves as though for the first time–
To the needy ten-year-old or with the dignified eyes of a centenarian-survivor–
Is a marvel because everyday images have the quality
Of diamonds that shine with crystals of gratitude
Or lustrous karats of piety.

El mundo enjoyado

La vida pasa en un lugar de zafiros:
Vea a los pétalos del jacinto de la primavera debutante;
Mire al cielo con su arco iris después de la lluvia del verano maduro;
Goze el azul mediterráneo desde la Riviera de la Bardot
Hasta los desfiles alocados de Tel Aviv –
Con sus éxtasis divinos y turquesas.

La vida pasa en un lugar de esmeraldas:
Vea a la hierba profusa de una colonia campestre de los Catskills;
Mire a las coníferas imponentes que fueron los padres confiables de
Hansel y Gretel;
Goze de las hojas del sauce que hacen reverencia y acarician a un lago
de menta.

La vida pasa en un lugar de ojo de gato:
Vea los campos marrones y cremas de la Tierra Sagrada;
Mire a la turba antigua y oscura donde jugaron los duendes en sus trajes
de oro;
Goze de los caballos árabes de ébano galopando sobre las arenas
De un desierto que habría sido abandonado si no fuera por sus cascos
desafiantes.

El mundo enjoyado en que nos encontramos como si fuese la primera vez–
A la desamparada edad de diez o con los ojos dignos de un centenario
superviviente –
Es una maravilla porque las imágenes de cada día tienen la calidad
De diamantes que brillan con los cristales de gratitud
Y los lustrosos quilates de la piedad.

Holy Land Species Villanelle

Stay battle axes before date palms' gentle sway;
Let three-year pomegranate saplings keep crimson crowns –
Bow down to gnarled olive roots—thousand-year display!

Sit in shade of fig tree, savoring sun's muted rays;
Contemplate trellised purple grapes that abound –
Stay battle axes before date palms' gentle sway!

Springtime barley harvest: for gleaning's romantic ways;
Mature, golden summer wheat: glimmering surrounds –
Bow down to gnarled olive roots—thousand-year display!

Pray for perfect citrons Moroccan farmers assay;
Gather jugs of white, rosé, garnet for toasts all 'round –
Stay battle axes before date palms' gentle sway!

Plant goodly carob — coax Messiah's soul-quenching stay;
Drizzle honey over aleph bet: child's first sounds –
Bow down to gnarled olive roots — thousand-year display!

Date palm is the giving tree: treat, beam, sieve, rope, tray –
Every part contributes, just like Moses' crowd.
Stay battle axes before date palms' gentle sway!
Bow down to gnarled olive roots — thousand-year display!

TREASURED EVERYWHERE

THE GODLY GINGKO TREE !

The Godly Gingko

Gingko tree:
Leaves like serrated fans
Caused Goethe to wonder,
"Are you two in one, or one in two?"
Male has spiraling cones resembling tousled maidenhair;
Female's flax-colored seeds teamed with coconut flesh
Make a tasty Thai dessert.

Fern-like essence from the Eocene –
Before flowers graced the Chinese landscape –
Your extract is a friend to human mental agility.
Longevity allows certain broad-crowned arbor to boast
Familiarity with Buddha, Confucius and tender hands of
Shrine-builders in Shinto Japan,
Tibetan monks eager for your aroma of intense greenness
In springtime and summer.

In autumn, your golden shimmer casting dappled leaf-shadows
Has been appreciated by Europe's Enlightenment philosophers,
America's first cultivated Captains of Industry,
And a denizen of Queens who has spied two males planted on either side
Of a Utopia Parkway driveway.

Why did six of your noble kind survive the Hiroshima bombing,
Rejuvenating from charred to healthy over the gentle, cherry blossom years?
Perhaps because there can be no return to Eden
Without the gingko.

In Praise of the Passerine

(Inspired by the sparrows of Whitestone and the hymn, "His Eye Is on the Sparrow")

Tsippor: Tzip, tzip, chirp, twitter, chatter!
Build a nest in a vineyard keeper's straw hat as resourceful passerines are wont to do;
Provide a humble gleaner's two-farthing Temple sacrifice of thanksgiving;
Chase away leprosy by giving your blood for a holy scattering;
Make orchard, field, garden and wall with crannied eaves your refuge;
Remember that the rooftops you roost upon are Godly altars.

Tsippor: Tzip, tzip, chirp, twitter, chatter!
Save Brooklyn trees from worm-death as you nourish famished chicks;
Prey on insects to cleanse the air for lovers spooning on darkened verandas;
Alight on air conditioners to charm city dwellers with your brown-gray attire;
Hop on a clothesline to do a cakewalk of puffy roundness;
Cajole your mate with self-assured whistles while weaving goldenrod into a welcoming oval cradle.

Sparrow, bring blessings to weary eyes that feast on your everyday presence;
Foster humility in creatures that bray and brag — not knowing that they are merely arrogant stardust;
Give comfort when the well-meaning powerful seek a Grace elusive as an orange oak leaf;
Peep choruses of cherry blossom glory with equal fervor before the flawed mighty and virtuous meek!

Trill-trill-trill avian arias,
Then spread white-tipped tail feather-fan for a flight that teaches about

Petite, muted beauty.

Tsippor: Tzip, tzip, chirp, twitter, chatter…

Unicorn and the Herd of Mustangs

(Inspired by Pearl Hochstadt's translation of *The Fables of La Fontaine*,
Books 1 –VI)

Unicorn found himself in the Wyoming plains,
Where he made small-talk with a herd of wild mustangs.
First he declared, "Fellow equines, we have manes
For tossing, four swift legs, a tail that flicks and hangs,
Muscular haunches, swan-grace necks, ears that stand and
Velvety mouths yearning for sugar cubes or carrots –
Not to mention large peepers for spying choice lands;
Noses that quiver, with skin as soft as rabbits."
Replied the leader of the wild mustang herd,
"This screed of brotherhood I'd find a pretty ditty,
If that horn between your ears were not so absurd!"
Each mustang concurred, letting out a "Whinny!"

Unicorn trotted off, away from hostile turf:
He'd be a herd of one, just as Maker had meant –
Ideals may be as fleeting as hoof prints in the surf;
Species-love as rare as four leaf clover forage spent.

VI. URBAN VIBES

Strawberry Fields Reverie

Today there is a lone sunflower
Gracing the center of the IMAGINE
John Lennon mandala.
In American summer attire
Of t-shirts, shorts, sneakers or sandals
An array of ages and ethnicities
Crouch in the middle
Respectfully, wistfully, joyously
While relatives or friends
Snap sublime photos.
Two brothers, two sisters,
Graying "esposo guapo"
Proudly extending wedding band hand,
Two friends — teen belles in blue jean short shorts,
Blissful college-age peace-beaded couple
Clasping hands in July sunshine –
All place themselves in brotherhood and sisterhood's
Rainbow crucible.
A gray-suited blond troubadour plays guitar,
Displaying a sign for "CD $5."
A Russian-speaking Adonis explains the meaning
Of this sacred checkerboard
To visiting parents more at home strolling
Onion-domed Red Square:
They, too, enter the tender vortex
Of permanent universal détente.

Five and Three in the City

Sam at five wears Museum of Natural History dinosaur classification t-shirt,
Flies plastic winged pterodactyl in U.N. Millennium Hotel West Wing room,
Zooms toy yellow Big Apple taxi cab forward and backward;
Pow! Pow! Pow! of karate chops and kicks are delivered like a black belt master.
In Great-Grandma Sarah's normally sedate Whitestone backyard
He cracks broad red bat to baseball with home run force again and again.
"Sam, would you bang against an ambassador's room with your red bat?"
"No, I wouldn't!"
"Sam, Great-Grandma Sarah didn't bring her bathing suit. Should she jump
in the hotel pool with her clothes on?
"Yes!"
Sam at five in the city shows both propriety and whimsy.

Abby at three is proud of her red-trimmed bathing suit –
She turns around like a model to show images of clocks and table lamps
That will surely charm families at the hotel pool.
Pink sandals, purple jump rope, blue-orange striped hula-hoop:
All are feminine accessories –
Not to mention beguiling light brown Shirley Temple curls.
Abby's "Blue Ribbon Bunny" dance routine is so graceful and endearing–
It could even disarm a demanding Ziegfeld Follies talent scout!
"Abby, should great-grandma jump into the hotel pool in her regular clothes?"
"No!"
Abby will be a sensible, protective balabusta someday.

Unlovely Proverbs

(Inspired by *Traces of Sepharad: Etchings of Judeo-Spanish Proverbs* by Marc Shanker)

Live in a metropolis, warm yourself with a torn patchwork quilt.

An untrustworthy friend changed from thoroughbred to donkey.

Mothers-in-law act like diamonds, but their true value is like rings of glass.

Spit in a fool's eye — he thinks it's eye drops.

Better to phone in sick for the day than to allow the boss's stooge to see you playing "Words with Friends" on a blackberry.

Better to pretend to be a fool than to allow a fox to outwit you.

Make your pace faster than the tortoise and slower than the squirrel.

Make your charity too generous for the miserly man and too tight for the spendthrift woman.

Refranes no preciosos

(Alentado a *Huellas De Sefarad*: aguafuertes de refranes judeo-español por Marc Shanker)

Vive en una metrópoli, se calienta con un edredón mosaico rasgado.

Un amigo indigno de confianza cambió de pura sangre a burro.

Las suegras se comportan como son los diamantes, pero sus valores exactas son como los anillos de vidrio.

Escupe en el ojo de un idiota — él cree que es el colirio.

Mejor llamar por teléfono, "¡Estoy enfermo hoy!" que permitir el monigote del jefe verte jugando "Las palabras con los amigos" en una mora.

Mejor fingir ser un imbécil que dejar un zorro ser más listo que usted.

Haga su ritmo menos lente que la tortuga y menos rápida que la ardilla.

Haga su caridad demasiado generosa para el avaro y demasiado ajustada para la despilfarradora.

Yiddish Family Traditions Abecedarian *

Alteh trombanick – *old bum*

Bist mushugeh? – *Are you crazy?*

Chaloshes – *loathsome*

Draykop – *scatterbrain*

Eppes narrishkeit – *some foolishness*

Farbissener – *embittered one*

Groisseh gedilleh! – *Big deal!*

Heymish – *homelike*

Ich vais nit! – *I don't know!*

Juli – *July*

Kakameyme – *outlandish*

Lemechel – *meek one*

Maideleh – *sweet little girl*

Nebechel – *a pitiful nothing*

Oyf tsu lehakhes! – *For spite!*

Prost – *coarse and rude*

Qualifikatzyah – *qualification*

Rebbitsen – *rabbi's wife or overly pious woman*

Shmendrik – *nincompoop*

Tsedrait – *confused*

Untershmeichlen – *to butter up*

Verklempt – *overwhelmed*

"Wen der zun gibt men tsu tati, vainer baiden." – *"When the son gives to the father, both cry."*

Xenofobia – *xenophobia*

Yachneh – *gossiping woman*

Zayt gezunt! – *Stay well!*

* The above Yiddish words and expressions were taken from the *Modern English-Yiddish, Yiddish-English Dictionary* compiled by Uriel Weinreich,

and also culled from the online Glossary of Yiddish Words and Phrases at: http://www.pass.to and http://kehillatisrael.net/docs/yiddish/yiddish.htm. Thanks also go to my maternal grand-parents Morris and Lena Kurinsky and my mother Sarah Kurinsky Hantman for using some of these Yiddish words and expressions at home during conversational commentary so that they are not alien to my ears.

Neue Galerie: From Sublime to Diabolical*

> *"Degenerates are not always criminals, prostitutes, anarchists
> and pronounced lunatics; they are often authors and artists."*
> — Max Nordau, *Entartung (Degeneration)*, 1892-1893

9 AM:
Café Sabarsky opens.
Apricot crêpes, Viennese hot chocolate,
Walnut paneling, newspapers hung from wooden rods,
Booths with velvet cushioning that seem to burst with flora:
A green-gold-orange Garden of Eden!

11 AM:
Glory in cosmetics magnate Ronald Lauder's prize acquisition –
Gustav Klimt's brunette icon "Adele Bloch-Bauer."
Her Cleopatra countenance is swathed in glint
Of a gold-silver peacock cape that glimmers
Ethereal elegance of the sheltered fin-de-siècle
Mitteleuropa banker's daughter/salonière/art collector set.

11:15 AM:
Entartete Kunst: Degenerate Art.
Emil Nolde's "Nordic Expressionism" qualified –
See how eerie his "The Life of Christ" cycle is,
Graced by raven-haired ghouls who grasp and hang
(Though a young Goebbels couldn't help his wayward admiration).
Notice triangles and square fractures of Paul Klee's "Masked Red Jew"–
Defining cubism and Picasso's genius as damnable.
It is pleasant to experience Oskar Kokoschka's handsome stare:
The artist dabbed shimmering impressionist brushstrokes

In shades of blue and beige that pay homage to personhood,
Rather than Alps or Danube.
What title has this lovely man chosen?
"Self-Portrait as a Degenerate Artist."
Now a series of full, frank portraits of the distinguished and accomplished
With thick or sharp features; round or thin, delicate physiques:
These works of George Grosz include "Portrait of John Forste, Man
with Glass Eye" –
This fellow reads a book, holds a cigarette with debonair nonchalance,
wears a smart brown suit and red tie –
Why should he be compelled to meet idyllic classical standards of pro-
portion and perfection
Inherited from Olympic Greece and Imperial Rome?
The pathos of Low German sculptor Ernst Barlach is not to be missed:
A frustrated bronze "Berserker" strains and pulls in two different directions;
A ceramic "Blind Beggar"—eyes heavenward—petitions and importunes;
"Mother and Child" with ancient Mongolian features nest and cuddle.
Jewish art dealer Alfred Flechtheim was in ecstasy over Barlach's ten-
derhearted oeuvre,
But how did this sculptor perceive the Establishment's reaction in 1937?
"Violent vomiting over me" was hard to accept as sculpted public monuments
Of this "pariah" were taken down and purposely damaged.
What was his stubborn conclusion from such a fall from favor?
Right was, is, and will remain right.
The order to bend it can never occur…
I am not in the slightest repentant or even improved."

Exit the Neue Galerie to glory in blessed late June afternoon sunshine;
Sit on a Central Park bench donated by gentle grandchildren in honor
of their beloved Nana;
Hope and hope that one's eight full-length books of verse filled with

themes of family, romance, faith, heritage, friendship, nature and nobility vs. evil
Qualify as "Entartete Kunst"!

* Stanza three observations were gleaned from the Neue Galerie exhi-
bition, "Degenerate Art: The Attack on Modern Art in Nazi Germany,
1937" (March 13 - September 1, 2014) and the accompanying catalogue.

Urban Ethical Will

My child,
Heed this counsel when I am dust:
While vying for a taxi at 22nd & 3rd,
Defer to betters with gray hair, canes, arthritis —-
For these are marks of wisdom's bounty.
As for that hard-of-hearing waiter at the T-Bone Diner:
Did you have the gall to fret when he served run-of-the-mill rice pudding
Instead of mouth-watering bread pudding with raisins?
For shame, my scion!
Far better to stifle grumbles at the public table
Than to chastise he who has served grits, scrambled eggs and grilled cheese
With such aplomb for two score years — and more.
Would thou darest tweak the nose
Of the curly-haired blond tyke who ran over thy foot
With his red Kickboard Mini Kick scooter in Battery Park?
Such lack of forbearance
Will cause me to rise up from the dead as a new Messiah –
And change the inherited portion of thy idyllic suburban villa
To less than 51% majority.
This I will do with the conviction of Joshua's wall-weakening
Shofar blasts at Jericho –
A town where the "sleep-deprived" could never advance over
The "early to bed, early to rise" crowd
(Unlike your precious Gotham).

Outer-Borough Paradise

A stone's throw from the blue-gray Bronx-Whitestone Bridge
(With its placid East River ripple-views)
Is the humble Whitestone Shopping Center:
Buy a red cloth poppy from a smiling, wizened WWII veteran
in Iwo Jima cap
As, seated on a wooden bench outside Chase,
He salutes the November wind and your $1 contribution
Made to alleviate suffering of the IED/PTSD generation of VETS –
His grandchildren-in-arms.
Key Food's outdoor stacking of birch logs and shelves of pumpkins in
every size to please
Is autumn eye-candy that beguiles in a beige-brown-orange outer-bor-
ough spectrum.
When winter arrives, a retired expert furrier may set up shop on a
bench just before Christmas –
Hawking gorgeous velvet with mink, sable, ermine or fox earmuffs
Fit for a chilled Czarina on a budget.
After thaw sets in, bring a flora poem printed on lavender paper
To gregarious Richard of Cross Island Frame-Art –
Negotiate a fair price for a mint-green border
While he asserts that many of his customers, like you, work for the
NYC D.O.E.
In summer, buy fresh-picked purple-blush figs in a lunch bag
Sold from a bench-stall for a pittance by a Whitestone neighbor who
has tenderly
Coddled his tree with black plastic wrapping to get through a New
World Northern winter
So lacking in the plentiful sunshine and clarity of his beloved, native
Greek Isle.

This outer-borough Eden
Is the Whitestone Shopping Center –
A Queens paradise for halcyon self-expression.

About the Author

Barbara Hantman is a Phi Beta Kappa graduate of Queens College with a Master's Degree in Language Arts from Teachers College, Columbia University. Her nine books of adult verse (Edwin Mellen Press, Xlibris, Friesen Press, Dorrance Publishing) contain some poems in Spanish and Hebrew, and cover themes ranging from Jewish holiday celebrations to the beauties of nature. An illustrated children's book— *Be Glad Your Ears are What They Are!*—is available from Xlibris. Her poem "Grandma Lena" won Second Prize in the Nassau County Poet Laureate Society 2015 Poetry Contest.

Barbara is now retired from her role serving a generation of NYC Department of Education students, and spends her days assisting her feisty nonagenarian mom.